POUNDED BY POLITICS

Nine Tales Of Civic Butthole Diplomacy

CHUCK TINGLE

CONTENTS

POUNDED BY THE POUND: TURNED GAY BY THE SOCIOECONOMIC IMPLICATIONS OF BRITAIN LEAVING THE EUROPEAN UNION

I open my eyes slowly, trying my best to regain my bearings. I'm in my bedroom, dull sunlight streaming through the cracks of the nearby blinds and flickering across my face. Everything around me is easily recognizable, yet for some reason it all seems very different this morning.

I take account of my surroundings and myself. My name is Alex Liverbort and I'm twenty-five years old, I'm in my rented flat in the heart of London and I have a splitting headache.

All of this is true, yet I still feel somehow disassociated from my own body.

Plus, I'm hungover.

I stand up and realize now that my clothes are still on, meaning that I must have simply fallen flat on the bed and passed out at some point during the previous evening. When I catch a glimpse of myself in the mirror I see that my hair is disheveled and messy, my eyes red as they struggle to focus.

I pull open the door of my bedroom and head out into the living quarters to see what's what, immediately finding my roommate, Krissy Buttmore, sitting on the couch with her attention glued to the television.

"What happened last night?" I ask her, rubbing my eyes. "My head is killing me."

Krissy glances over, looking much less disheveled then me but just as distressed. "It's all going to hell," my roommate informs me bluntly.

"What is?" I question.

1

Krissy's expression quickly changes to one of confusion.

"I think I blacked out," I admit. "I have no idea what's going on."

My roommate's eyes go wide. "You don't remember the vote? Britain has decided to leave the European Union. Brexit, remember?"

Suddenly, it all comes flooding back. I remember watching at the local pub as the poll numbers came in, slowly but surly drowning out all hope that I had in a future as part of the EU.

My spirits crushed, I took to drinking. Everything else is a blur, but at some point I vaguely recall running down the block to the River Thames and throwing a bottle of wine into the water.

"So we're leaving the union?" I ask.

"Yep," Krissy confirms.

I let out a long sigh, then look past my friend, out through the open window of our second story apartment and onto the streets of London below. The usual folks are hustling and bustling about, continuing on their merry way as if nothing out of the ordinary had even happened.

"Seems like everything's... fine," I tell Krissy. I'm not exactly sure what I expected after my night of alcohol fueled depression and sociopolitical terror, but this isn't it.

"The pound is losing value fast," Krissy notifies me. "It's in free fall. The whole economy is bound to collapse."

I hear the words that she's saying, and I completely understand that they should strike even more fear into my heart, but for some reason they don't. Maybe all of the anger and frustration was purged from my system the night before, because right now I don't really feel much of anything.

"I'm gonna go for a walk," I tell my roommate, trying to make it sound like I've got some kind of emotional steam valve to let off, but really just not knowing what else to do with myself.

Without another word, I turn around and grab my coat, heading down the stairs and out onto the busy streets. I immediately take a left and head towards the river, to the same vague spot that I had somehow ended up the night before.

I can't help but notice how excruciatingly normal everything seems. Across the street two handsome men are walking a dog together, while a Kabob shop to my left serves up some hungry customers. I see busses, I see taxis, I see everything that I would expect to see despite these dire warnings of economic collapse.

When I finally reach the edge of the River Thames I find a nice quiet bench and take a seat, looking out across the deep blue water and to the seemingly endless grey sky above. While some people might find the dreariness of today unsettling, I find it deeply comforting, yet another sign that some things just never change.

Across the waves of the river I can see Parliament, and I can't help but wonder what kind of heads are rolling over there right now. I'm sure there is some kind of political chaos underway, but I'm certain it will work itself out.

Finally feeling connected to my own body once again, I lean back into the bench and let out a long sigh, closing my eyes as sweet relief washes over my body.

Suddenly, there is a deafeningly loud crackle of lighting in front of me, causing me to nearly fall out of my seat as I let out a cry of surprise. Floating some two or three feet above the sidewalk is a black and blue seam of electricity, a hovering slit in the fabric of space and time that pours outward with a sizzling heat.

"Alex!" calls a voice from beyond the strange universal rift. I can barely make out the figures shape, but it appears to be a massive, sentient coin; one pound to be exact.

"Hello?" I question, shielding my eyes from the electrical storm that appears to be occurring right before me. "Who are you?"

"There's no time!" yells the giant coin from the other side of the rift. "Come with me!"

I'm utterly horrified and, if I'm going to be honest, my first instinct is to immediately turn around and run away. It's only then that I notice something brilliant and burning through the hole in space-time. Within the rift I can see The Parliament, or what used to be The Parliament, as the entire building roars with a towering flame.

"Is that what it looks like?" I call out.

"Yes!" screams the giant sentient coin. "We need your help, Alex. I can't hold this open much longer!"

Suddenly, all of the fear leaves and is replaced with a powerful, frantic energy. Britain needs me!

Without another thought, I jump up from the bench and run forward, diving through the trans universal slice and ending up carried to a hellish landscape of fire and smoke on the other side.

"Where am I?" I ask this mysterious pound. "What's happening?"

"You're in the future," explains the giant sentient monetary instrument, "but it's not safe here. Follow me!"

The pound takes off floating along the edge of the River, which I now see is blood red and bubbling like the lava of a molten volcano. Many of the once familiar buildings are gone, while others still burn in behemoth pylons of flame. Strange creatures circle the sky in red uniforms with large black hats, dressed the Queen's Guard but with leathery reptilian wings and extended knifelike teeth.

"How long has it been?" I ask the living pound as we hustle along. "Seventy years? Eighty?"

"It's been a month," the sentient currency tells me.

"A month," I stammer, "but, how did this happen?"

Suddenly, bullets strike in rapid succession across the ground beside us, fired from above by one of the monstrous winged guardsmen.

"This way!" The floating coin shouts, leading me past the wreckage of a toppled four-story bus. The pound sees me looking at the strange vehicle and offers a quick explanation. "To make up for lost revenue we invested in four story busses instead of the traditional double-decker. They were too top heavy and started tipping over everywhere. It was utter panic in the streets."

"What about the guards?" I question.

"The government couldn't afford to pay the Queen's Guards anymore so we used these unfinished snake and bat hybrids that MI5 has been developing," explains the coin. "It was *not* a good idea."

"I can see that," I tell him. Of course, what I am most curious about is how the future managed to create a massive, living, breathing pound, but I say nothing.

Finally, the two of us find an abandoned pub to duck into, hidden from the strange uniformed monsters who circle menacingly in the dark sky above. The coin slams the door behind us and locks it, then staggers over to the bar and grabs a bottle from behind the counter, pouring himself a drink.

"You want some?" the living economic unit asks.

I nod. "Sure thing."

The coin pours two glasses and hands one to me, then takes a seat at a nearby table. I follow his lead, sitting in the chair across from him and taking a long sip from my glass. The pub is eerily quiet, utterly devoid of any patrons.

"What's your name?" I finally question, breaking the silence.

"Perber," offers the coin. "I already know yours, though."

"How?" I continue.

Perber pulls out a wine bottle from under the table and uncorks it, then lets a rolled up letter fall out between us. He unfurls it and hands it over to me. "Look familiar?" the sentient pound asks.

It doesn't, but I don't say anything, just take the page and read aloud. "Dear future Brits," I begin. "I'm so sorry, we really messed up. If anyone in the future finds this, please know that if I could go back and change the way things worked out, I would. Whoa, I'm so drunk right now. Oh well." I stop abruptly, finding my own name scribbled at the bottom.

"Do you remember writing that and tossing it in the river?" asks Perber.

I hesitate, and then finally decide to answer honestly. "I was pretty drunk."

The coin looks a little concerned but pushes that expression away as quickly as it arrives. He tries to change the subject. "So I'm sure you're wondering how we all became giant, floating coins, huh?" the pound asks me.

"Actually, yeah," I confess. "Did you just say *all*?"

The pound nods.

"As in, everyone became coins, not just you?" I continue.

"The pound lost so much value that we had to make up for it by becoming pounds ourselves," Perber explains.

"That doesn't really make any sense," I tell him.

"None of this makes any sense," the coin counters, "but it's all we've got left. *You're* all we've goy left."

I take a long sip from my drink, finishing the whole thing in one gulp and then slamming the glass down on the table. "What do you need me to do?" I question.

"You need to go back to the past and warn them," explains Perber. "We'll send you back months before the vote and you can get the word out; about the four story busses, the winged monsters, the living coins. They'll have no choice but to vote to stay in the European Union."

"I don't know if they're going to believe me," I inform the coin. "Besides, if I go back and prevent the vote from happening, then I won't know to come back and prevent it in the first place. It's a loop, it doesn't make any sense."

Perber shakes from side to side. "No, no," the living coin counters, "It just creates a new timeline. This one will still exist, but at least you'll be saving the others."

"Still," I argue, "nobody will believe me... unless you come back with me."

I see a twinkle in Perber's eye as he hears this. "You think?"

"Absolutely," I tell him, standing up from my chair with a renewed faith in our plan. "Alright, let's get started, how do we do this?"

"Love," explains the coin. "All you need is love."

I stand there in silence, just staring at Perber as I   wait for him to explain himself.

"We need to make love to each other," the coin continues.

"What?" I blurt, in utter shock.

The coin nods.

"Then how'd you come back and get me?" I question.

"That was love, as well," offers the living pound, "the love of my country. Love is the most powerful force in *any* universe, capable of transcending space and time. Unfortunately, I've already used that particular patriotic form of love. Now we need to harness a different kind."

None of this makes even the slightest bit of sense, but there is something about the way that this massive sentient pound carries himself that actually makes me kind of excited about the prospect of learning to love him. There is no denying just how handsome he is with that perfectly circular, ridged edge, and his flat golden surface that glints under the dim pub light. I've never experience sexual feelings for another male before, but right now there is no denying the way that my heart beat quickens, the way that I yearn for his powerful, monetary unit touch.

"I think you might be on to something," I finally offer, walking around the table and pressing myself up against the massive coin. I run my hands up and down across his cool surface, taking note of every subtle edge and texture.

My cock is quickly stiffening within my pants, growing harder and harder with every passing moment as I wallow in the presence of this beautiful currency.

Suddenly, I just can't help myself any longer. I drop to my knees and take the coin's cock in my hand, a thick golden rod that has somehow emerged from Perber's front.

"Whoa, look at that," I gush, taking in the massive size of his monetary rod.

I pump my hand up and down his length for a while, faster and faster as I go until finally I open wide and swallow the entire thing into my mouth. I wrap my lips around his cock and then push down as far as I can go, retching slightly as I hit the edge of my gag reflex and then pulling back with a stutter.

I try my best to collect myself, wiping the spit from my mouth as I give the coin a playful wink. "Sorry about that, this is my first time," I tell him. "I guess this socioeconomic disaster has had at least *one* upside… It's turned me gay."

My second attempt at a deep throat goes much better than the first. This time, I'm somehow able to relax enough to allow the sentient pound's massive rod all that way down to the hilt, stopping only when my face presses up hard against his incredible set of chiseled metallic abs.

Perber lets out a long, satisfied moan, tilted back as the sound vibrates through his entire body.

I love giving him pleasure, welcoming him into my body like he's welcomed me into this horrific timeline. I am here to guide him as he guides me, showing him the deepest darkest parts of my soul and baring it all.

When I've finally run out of air I pull back with an enormous gasp, aching to take things to the next level.

"I want you to fuck me," I tell the living coin. "I want you to fuck me up my tight gay ass, just like we've all fucked ourselves with this vote!"

Perber smiles. "With pleasure."

The coin helps lift me to my feet and then immediately spins me around with his powerful currency arms. He pushes me up to the bar and bends me over it roughly, tearing down my pants and underwear before aligning his massive dick with the tightly puckered rim of my exposed backdoor.

"Oh my god," I groan. "Pound me, pound! Just do it!"

The massive sentient coin teases me for a bit longer, playfully exploring the tension of my anal rim before finally pushing down inside of me in one long, powerful swoop.

I let out a deep, drawn out groan, my body struggling to adjust to the incredible size of his thick member. My asshole is completely stretched to the brink, feeling as though it's about to break in half as the incredible pound behind me starts to slowly move his hips.

He's allowing me to learn his cock, giving our bodies time to connect as he slowly but surely pumps faster into me. Eventually, all of the discomfort that I once felt while taking his massive rod has slipped away, evolving into something else entirely. Soon every thump of the coin against my backside sends a shiver of pleasure up my spine, the tightness of my butthole feeling full but not quite overwhelmed.

"Harder," I tell Perber, the words a little bit under my breath and then once more with feeling. "Harder!"

The living coin picks up his pace, moving even faster now as he slams against my backside in a ferocious haze of blinding lust.

"You like that?" Perber demands to know.

"Oh my god!" I scream, " I love being pounded by my pound!"

My hands gripping tightly onto the bar in front of me, I begin to push back against him, thrusting backwards just as hard as he's pummeling up into my ass. My eyes roll back in my head and I reach down between my legs, grabbing ahold of my hanging cock and beginning to beat myself off in time with his movements.

Soon enough, I can feel myself approaching the edge of orgasm, but before I have a chance to make it there the handsome coin pulls out of me and gives me a hard slap on the ass.

"Over here," the sentient currency commands. The coin lies down flat against the bar floor, the only relief on his otherwise even surface a massive tower dick that he coaxes me over to.

I do as I'm told, approaching the handsome pound as I remove the rest of my clothing, tossing it to the side as I come to a stop over the enormous circular object. Carefully, I lower myself down into a squat, aligning my butthole with the pound's enormous cock and then, eventually, impaling myself along his length. Even though I'm the one doing the moving here, I still let out a surprised yelp as Perber's shaft enters me, not entirely accustomed to his thick British banger.

Now I'm riding him, swooping my body across the pound's flat surface in a series of firm movements of the hip. My cock bounces in front of me with every slam, hard but wild as it twirls in the air like a helicopter.

"Our love transcends space and time!" I cry out. "Love is all you need! Love is all you need!"

Faster and faster I go, riding the living monetary instrument with everything I've got. It's not long before I feel a strange and unfamiliar sensation begin to boil up from somewhere deep inside of me, simmering just below the surface as it begins to make it's way through my veins. I feel as though I'm about to cum harder than I ever have in my life, but not in the same old way that I've grown accustomed to. This is something different, something much more *anal*.

"Oh god, my fucking prostate," I moan, finally realizing what this bizarre sensation is. "I'm gonna cum! Keep hitting that prostate deep in this tight gay asshole!"

Harder and harder I bounce on the coin, losing myself in the overwhelming sensation until, suddenly, it's just too much to hold back any longer. I find myself blasting across the pound's shiny surface. Load after load ejects from the head of my shaft, spilling out onto Perper in a beautiful display of pearly white spunk that splatters this way and that. My teeth clenched tight, I hiss though the opening as my body struggles to understand all of this sensation.

Finally, the feelings pass and I collapse back onto the floor behind me, sweaty and exhausted.

The coin immediately stands up and looms over my muscular body, spreading my legs open and positioning himself before me.

"I love you," Perper admits, tears of joy in his eyes, "and I want to cum inside of you."

"Please," I tell him, a wry smile on my face as I reach down and spread my reamed asshole open.

Perber wastes no time slipping inside and getting to work, picking up right where he left of with a powerful pound pounding. He hammers away at me with staggering enthusiasm and then suddenly pushes down as deep as he can go, holding in place while letting out a rumbling groan of pleasure. I can feel his warm coin spunk spill out into my ass, filling me up to the brim and then spilling out from the edges of my tightly plugged butthole.

When the sentient pound finally finishes he removes himself from me, letting a torrent of jizz come tumbling after. It runs down the crack of my ass and onto the pub floor, pooling out around us in a beautiful mess.

The pool doesn't stop growing, however, seeping out across the floor below in an ever expanding puddle of jizz that soon begins to crackle and snap with sizzling electrical energy.

"It's happening!" Perber shouts excitedly. "Our love is real!"

"Of course it is," I tell him with a wide smile, throwing my arms around the coin and pulling him close. "No matter what happens, I'll always love you."

Suddenly, the air of the room changes completely, the creeping silence and dread replaced by the warm din of a humming tavern. I look up to see that we are surrounded by men and women in the heat of conversation, but the second that they see me and my coin lover, everyone stop to stare.

The music that had once been filling the air comes screeching to an abrupt halt.

"What in the fuck," someone finally says, breaking the silence.

"Listen to me," I tell the crowd, springing into action. "My friend and I have come from the future to warn you about the upcoming vote to leave the European Union."

"The what?" comes the same drunken voice.

"The European Union," I repeat. "Brexit!"

"Who the fuck cares," says the man. "We need to stop them mainlanders from coming into our country, anyway."

I shake my head, trying to reason with them. "You don't understand, it's all going to fall apart. It's complete chaos. We need to stay. Don't let your hatred blind you."

"Fuck off!" another voice shouts.

"Yeah, get outta here with that nonsense!" someone else chimes in. "I don't want any damn foreigners coming in here and mucking stuff up for us *real* Brits."

More and more angry patrons add their voice to the ruckus, silencing my plea for peace and acceptance.

Suddenly, a loud whistle cuts through the chaos. Once more, the bar falls into a silence as Perber steps forward to address the drunken mob.

"All you need is love," the coin suddenly sings out.

Silence.

"All you need is love," the handsome coin repeats.

More silence.

Perper hesitates, then changes his approach ever so slightly. "All you need is butts," he sings once more.

Suddenly, I see tonight's pub crawlers take notice, the men and women perking up slightly as these words resonate just the tiniest bit more.

"All you need is butts!" one of the drunks yells back in refrain.

Suddenly, the whole pub is singing along as loud as they can, belting out the words like their life depended on it. After another rousing chorus, Perber climbs up onto one of the tables and addresses the gathering.

"We're a fantastic country, with a rich heritage," announces the living pound, "but being a part of the European Union doesn't take away from what makes us Brits. In fact, the EU just means that there are even more butts to go around!"

"Yeah!" replies the crowd enthusiastically.

"German butts, French butts, Spanish butts!" Perber cries out. "There's no end to the variety when you open your heart's butt to your neighbors! So when it comes time to vote, let's keep our asses wide open!"

The entire pub explodes in a cheer of excitement as a warm smile slowly begins to creep out across my face.

Perper climbs down off of the table and then walks back over to me, the crowd now caught up in excited conversations of their own. The coin takes me in his arms and kisses me deeply.

When we pull away, I can't help asking him what all of this means for the future.

"I have no idea," the handsome pound admits, "but it's a good start."

"All you need is… butts?" I question.

"*Love* is the real answer," Perber explains, "you know it, I know it. Sometimes it takes butts to get peoples attention, though. I have faith that they'll look even deeper and understand the real meaning."

"You sure about that?" I question.

"There's only one way to find out," the sentient coin says with a laugh.

FEELING THE BERN IN MY BUTT

Politics have always been something that I avoided, mostly because every time I try to get involved I just end up getting too pissed off to continue. Not just pissed off by the opposing side, but by the side that I support, as well. Honestly, it's a little exhausting, and even though I've only been able to vote in a single election cycle thus far in my young life as a twenty-something, I'm not sure that it's something I ever want to do again.

I suppose this is what everyone's feeling these days, though. The disenchantment with American government runs deep on both sides of the aisle. To be a front-runner in this race, the one thing that you need to be is an outsider.

This is why I never expected to have my entire life turned upside down by a political candidate the way that it was on that fateful afternoon, to have my life forever changed by a single, beautiful man.

I'm watching TV in the living room of my small, two-bedroom apartment on a Saturday afternoon. It's been a long workweek and, while I would normally be spending what little free time I have running around and taking care of errands, I'm just too exhausted at this point. I need to chill.

Honestly, these days I feel like all that I do is work, forced to take on more and more hours of overtime just to make ends meet. The minimum wage here is so low that, even in an office as nice as mine, I can barely afford to keep a roof over my head.

The television suddenly cuts to the afternoon news, the staccato intro music catching my attention as a large channel-five logo flies across the screen.

"Senator Bernie Sambers is now catching up in the Democratic Primaries," announces the newscaster. "The presidential hopeful was once seen as a long shot but has been gaining serious momentum over the last couple of weeks. As of this morning, he's here in California holding rallies and getting ready for this weekends vote."

I'd heard a little bit about Bernie Sambers, but not enough to quell the immediate gagging sensation I feel at yet another slimy politician scrambling for my vote.

I hear the apartment door open behind me as my roommate, Bipper, arrives home.

"Can you believe this guy?" I call over to Bipper, gesturing towards the screen.

My roommate walks over and glances at the TV, a look of immediate recognition crossing his face.

"You don't like Bernie?" he asks. "I'm surprised."

I scoff. "What do you mean? All politicians are the same, just a bunch of rich scumbags taking away from the little guy."

Bipper chuckles. "Honestly, I don't think you're right about Bernie this time."

I roll my eyes.

"Seriously, Lorp" Bipper continues. "I'm headed down to the rally later, you should come with me. Check it out for yourself."

At first I'm not sure if he's being serious, figuring this is some kind of dry sarcastic bit that I just haven't picked up on yet, but as our gaze holds I slowly begin to realize that Bipper is for real.

"Alright," I finally say, cautiously.

Bipper smiles and pats me on the shoulder. "I think you're going to like this."

The second that we enter the arena downtown I can tell that this isn't your typical political gathering. Every sign that I see has a message that resonates deeply within me, deeper than any candidate has ever been able to reach. While most politicians craft messages that tug at my heartstrings, these seem to go even father. He's tugging at my butt.

"Are you feeling the burn?" my roommate leans over and asks me. "Are you feeling the burn in your butthole?"

I check in with myself, considering his words for a moment. I have to admit, all of this political positivity is getting to me, the message of progress and social reform causing a pleasant tingle to slowly form around the rim of my anus. It's a strange but welcome sensation, something of a burn, but in a warm and inviting way.

"This is... amazing," I tell my friend, the blissful sensation suddenly flowing out from my butthole and across my entire body until it reaches my heart. It is a numbing ache, a tension that seems to playfully tease both my rectum and my soul.

We make our way through the crowd and into the packed arena, which usually hosts basketball games but has been rented out for the evening. The lights are dim and music thumps through the overhead speakers, creating an air of excitement. Before us, there is a massive stage draped with American flags, where a spotlight centered downward upon a dark wooden podium.

"Just in time," Bipper says as the lights dim even more.

Suddenly, the crowd begins to roar, their cheers and thunderous applause eventually morphing into one singular auditory sensation, as if we've all come together as a single entity.

"Ladies and gentlemen," an announcer begins, his voice reminding me of the man who calls out boxing or wrestling matches, "Bernie Samberrrrrrrrrrrssssss!"

Suddenly, showers of red white and blue sparks erupt from the stage, creating glorious fountains of light that glimmer out across the darkness above. From somewhere behind the hanging flags comes a stark white, galloping figure, his wintery mane flowing out behind him and the horn on his head shimmering brilliantly; Bernie Sambers.

He's old and slightly hunched, with glasses and a bald spot on the top of his head, yet there is something strangely alluring about this man's physical presence that I can't quite put my finger on. Something just doesn't add up.

I lean over to Bipper. "Is Bernie a... human?" I ask him.

"A human?" my friend counters.

"Yeah, like, remember when it came out that Domald Tromp was a dinosaur?" I question.

"Sure," offers Bipper.

"Do you think something like that could be happening with Bernie?" I continue. "There's just something *strange* about him, something magical."

"That's the magic of democracy!" Bipper cries out. "The magic of someone finally representing the people!"

I nod and turn my attention back to the stage, still unable to shake the feeling that something peculiar is going on with this supernaturally alluring politician. There's something about his horn, and the way that he prances about on the stage before me, that just seems a bit odd.

One things for sure, though, he's a hell of a speaker. Over the next hour we're treated to the most powerful political call to arms that I have ever witnessed. The entire crowd is utterly enchanted by his uncanny charm, hanging on every word as the presidential hopeful lays out his glorious plan for a better tomorrow. At one point a tiny bird actually flutters down and lands on the podium, listening intently to Bernie's speech as a representative of the natural world. Soon enough, more and more animals start to join the bird, every woodland creature imaginable approaching the stage and taking a seat at the edge. Deer, rabbits and foxes all make an appearance, and finally even a large brown bear arrives to take it all in.

Bernie is unfazed by this appearance of wild creatures, not turning them away but instead welcoming them gladly into the mob of feverish supporters.

By the end of the speech, I find myself fully converted to the Sambers cause. This is not just another run-of-the-mill politician, this is someone who has true heart and wants to make a real change within the political system.

"Thank you!" the candidate yells out across the audience, throwing his hands up and turning to walk away from the microphone.

I'd been so enraptured in his words that I'd completely lost focus on just how much time had passed.

"Is that it?" I gasp, as if suddenly coming up for air from under a breaking wave.

Bipper shakes his head and then cracks a smile. "Oh no, not quite," my friend tells me. "Bernie is a man of the people, he's going to be in the lobby handing out fresh backed cookies."

I laugh a little as Bipper says thi,s until I realize that he's not joking. Soon enough, we are following the crowd out into the arena hallway where a long line of supporters have gathered to accept piping hot chocolate chip cookies from the man himself.

"We've gotta get some," I gush, hopping in line immediately.

Somehow we've found ourselves right up front, and from this close I can once again see that something is quite unusual about Bernie Sambers.

It's not long before we make it to the front of the line.

"Thank you, that was an amazing speech," I tell him. "You've got yourself a new supporter after that."

Bernie cracks a playful smile as he locks eyes with me, and immediately I can sense a strong tingling in my butthole, a powerful sizzling sensation that courses through my loins like an electric current.

"I'm glad to hear it!" Bernie replies. He reaches out his hand to shake mine and, the second I take it, I get another strange feeling. I look down, realizing that what I'm holding is actually a large hoof, and then pull away.

"You seem like a nice young man," Bernie Sambers tells me. "Could you stick around for a moment after all of this is finished?"

"Me?" I question, taken completely off guard.

"If you're friend doesn't mind," Bernie continues, nodding towards Bipper.

"Not at all," my roommate assures the politician. "Whatever I can do to help the campaign."

"Good," says Bernie, turning his attention back to me. "My people will take care of you until then. I'll be back to speak with you shortly."

The next thing I know, two large men in black suits have approached on either side. I know that they're simply there to escort me into a private area, but I can't help being intimidated by their incredible size.

"Right this way," one of the body guards says.

I give Bipper a quick wave and then allow the guards to lead me away from the crowd off down the hallway and behind a thick curtain. Suddenly, all of the chaos has morphed into a strange, surreal silence; the only noise that remains is the clicking of our feet as we walk through the empty foyer.

"In here," one of the guards offers, leading me to a door and then opening it up and waving me inside.

During basketball games this part of the arena is probably used for storing equipment or something equally banal, but tonight things are completely different. An assortment of ornate rugs and tapestries have been brought in to furnish the place, their red, white and blue fabrics draped everywhere while an assortment of satin loungers lie placed about.

I take a seat on one of them, trying to relax as I savor the flavor of my delicious chocolate chip cookies. Despite the rather patriotic color scheme in here, there is also something vaguely sensual about the décor. I hadn't noticed it until now, but I can faintly make out the sound of a smooth jazz national anthem cover floating down from somewhere above me.

Feeling sufficiently relaxed, I lean back into the lounger and close my eyes, letting a heavy wave of calm wash over me.

"You're exactly the kind of voter that we're looking for in this campaign," a voice suddenly cuts through the darkness of my mind.

My eyes fly open and I sit up, realizing now that I had somehow managed to fall asleep. I'm still backstage at the arena, sitting in the ornately decorated room. Now, however, a guest has joined me.

"Bernie," I say aloud, recognizing the man immediately.

The presidential hopeful smiles, sending a sharp chill down my spine and up my butt.

"That's me," he replies, "and you are?"

"Lorp," I explain, "it's nice to meet you."

"It's nice to meet you, too," Bernie Sambers tells me. The man stands up from his seat across the room and slowly walks over to me, his hips swaying from side to side with a little more kick than seems natural. If I didn't know any better I would say that he's trying to seduce me, not that I would mind.

Bernie sits down next to me on the lounger and then places a hand on my knee. Strangely, I don't have even the slightest desire to pull away, I just flick my eyes over towards him in a playful gesture of acceptance.

"Why did you want me to come back here?" I question. "Why me?"

The democratic candidate looks deep into my eyes, his gaze searing down into the most private recesses of my soul. "Because I saw something in you," he tells me.

"What?" I ask, my voice trembling. "What did you see?"

"My running mate," Bernie tells me.

My heart skips a beat as he says this, my mind struggling to accept the unexpected but very welcome turn of events. "Me?" I question. "I'm not qualified for that."

"You're more than qualified," Bernie assures me. "Those eyes, that muscular chest." The candidate places his hand against my pectorals and lets it drift slowly downward. "You're exactly what we're looking for. I knew from the second that I saw you, you'd be the perfect vice president."

"I don't know what to say," I tell him.

Bernie smiles. "Well, don't get too excited yet," he counters. "We still need to vet you."

Bernie's palm reaches my crotch as he says this and he immediately grips me with a firm handful of balls and shaft through the fabric. I sit straight up, my eyes going wide and my body trembling.

"Would you like me to vet you?" Bernie coos. "Would you like me to get deep down in there and see what I can find?"

"Yes," I moan.

The politician begins to unbutton my fly, and yet again I notice something strange about his hands, something not quite human.

"Wait," I say, stopping him in his tracks. "If you're going to vet me, I need to vet you. There's something you're hiding."

Bernie lets out a long sigh. "You can tell, can't you? Is it that obvious?"

I shake my head. "No, it's not. I don't know what's going on with you, but something is up. How is it that you're such a perfect candidate? You never flip-flop, you never mess up; it's like you're made of magic or something."

"I *am* made of magic," Bernie tells me. "I'm a unicorn."

Suddenly, the horn, the hooves and the mane all make perfect sense. I have no idea how I was unable to connect the dots before this, but now that I've seen the light there is no turning back. Bernie is a unicorn; a glorious, muscular, white-haired unicorn, and he's sexy as fuck.

Suddenly, I'm completely overwhelmed with arousal. I grab the unicorn and pull him towards me, kissing him deeply on the mouth as my hands roam across his beautifully toned body. They drift lower and lower until eventually they grab ahold of Bernie's rock hard unicorn cock.

"Oh fuck," the mythical beast groans as I stroke his shaft, slowly at first and then eventually speeding up with every pump. I slip down off of the lounger so that I'm kneeling before him, his massive political cock jutting out towards my face like a flagpole on the Fourth of July.

Without thinking twice, I open up wide and take Bernie's dick between my lips, immediately shocked by the incredible taste. I was fully expecting a subtle, salty flavor to his manhood, but instead I'm greeted by a sensual explosion of taste that shifts between cotton candy, bubblegum and cherry. This man can truly do no wrong.

Eventually, I push down as far as I can and hold, taking the unicorn politician's beastly manhood within my wet mouth. His cock dives deeper and deeper, sinking past the limits of my gag reflex until finally stopping when I reach the hilt. I find my face pushed up against Bernie's magical, sparkling abs,

The unicorn throws his head back and let's out another long groan, this one even more powerful that the first. I can tell that I am giving him real, genuine pleasure, servicing him expertly despite the fact that I'm completely straight and this is the first gay experience of my life.

When I finally pull back I erupt off of him in a shower of spit. I gasp loudly and struggle to collect myself, my senses a blur of new and exciting eroticism. I hadn't even noticed until now, but I suddenly realize my butthole is tingling once more, not just the soft, sizzling surges, but a full-on rattle that courses through my body and causes me to tremble wildly.

"I can feel the burn in my butthole," I tell him. "It's incredible."

"You ain't felt nothing yet," Bernie retorts.

At first I'm not quite sure what that means, but as soon as the massive unicorn starts to guide me into position I get the idea. Bernie pushes me forward so that I'm now on the floor on my hands and knees, my ass popped out behind me as I give it a playful wiggle. I reach back and pull down my pants and underwear, exposing my tight butthole to the magical creature.

"Do it," I tell him, "ram me up the ass the filthy little voter twink that I am!"

Bernie smiles and then begins to position himself, but not in the way that I expected.

"What's going on?" I stammer, looking back over my shoulder.

"You trust me with your vote," the unicorn laughs, "don't you trust me with your butt?"

I swallow hard and then nod, happy to push my sexual boundaries yet anxious about this wholly new experience. Up until this point I had never even considered a gay encounter, straight as they come and completely satisfied as such. Now, however, I'm not so sure.

Bernie leans his head down behind me and aligns the tip of his shimmering ivory horn with my butthole, teasing the rim as he explores the limits of my tightness.

"Oh my god," I moan, "that feels so fucking good. Just do it, shove that big, fat unicorn horn up into my ass!"

With that, the presidential hopeful pushes forward, slowly but firmly as he expands the limits of my sphincter around his beautiful horn. Deeper and deeper he slides until the protrusion is fully inserted within my anus, literally humming with political energy as though an electrical current is pulsing through it.

I can feel the democratic socialist vibrations filling my ass with warmth and then spilling out across my body, running down my arms and legs in a series of pleasant waves. Most importantly, I can feel the way that they massage my prostate deep within, causing my muscles to clench and release at the first hints of orgasm.

"Feel that burn!" Senator Sambers begins to command. "Feel that burn! Feel that fucking burn!"

"I feel it!" I scream in return. "This ass is for the people not just the wealthy elite!"

"Yes!" Bernie cries out enthusiastically.

The unicorn is pumping his horn in and out of me now, faster and faster as the incredible stimulation builds. My cock is rock hard, and I reach down between my legs to grip it tightly. I pump my hand across my length in time with the horned hammers against my backside, reeling from the incredible sensation. I can feel the orgasm within blossoming larger and larger, growing until I'm almost entirely consumed by its aching tension.

Just as I'm about to finish, however, Bernie removes his magical horn from my anus.

"Oh fuck," I groan. "I was so close."

"Climb on," the unicorn tells me with a wink.

I stand up, fully removing my clothes and then approaching the magical creature. I start to climb onto his back but Bernie stops me.

"No, down there," he instructs.

I'm confused at first, but then vaguely begin to understand as the unicorn lifts one leg to allow me underneath.

"Oh, I see," I giggle, climbing below and wrapping my naked body around Bernie's undercarriage. I can feel his massive cock tickling the rim of my already reamed out backdoor, and I instinctively push myself down, impaling my body across his mammoth rod.

"Hang on," Bernie says mischievously, then begins to gallop towards the door. We hit it hard, bursting through and out into the arena hallway yet again.

It's late in the evening now, but there are still a few supporters milling about. When they see us they start to cheer, immediately recognizing this moment for what it is, the official announcement of Bernie Sambers vice presidential running mate.

"I am pleased to say that Lorp Rims is my new running mate!" the unicorn bellows as we gallop past the onlookers, the cock still slamming away at my asshole.

The people erupt in cheer as we fly by, rocketing down the hallway and out through the doors of the arena.

The city streets are packed with people who all turn to look in awe at these two magical political figures tearing down the sidewalk. I'm completely overwhelmed by the pounding of my anus, but not enough to miss the long magical streak of red white and blue that extends out behind us.

"Your new vice president!" Bernie is shouting, his words echoing through the city streets.

Overhead, news helicopters have started to swarm, their cameras pointing down at us as they project this historic gay event across the world.

Eventually, Bernie and me end up at the steps of city hall, we're we slow to a stop and the incredible, muscular politician pulls his dick out of me. I let go of his beautiful white body and drop down onto the steps, realizing now that we are utterly surrounded with enthusiastic supporters.

Then begin to chant, but instead of the typical cries for "Bernie" I hear my own name being repeated over and over by the seemingly endless throngs. "Lorp! Lorp! Lorp!" they chant.

The unicorn stands over me now, beating off his massive cock as I stretch out before him. He is seizing with pleasure, aching to blow his pent up political load all over me.

I reach down between my legs and begin to stroke along with him, furiously pulsing my tightly gripped hand across my length.

"I'm gonna cum," I start to murmur, the volume of the crowd growing all around us. "I'm gonna fucking cum!"

"Me too!" says Bernie.

Suddenly, the unicorn senator throws his head back and lets out a long, satisfied moan. His cock twitches and then flings a series of hot, white ropes out across my chest and abs, raining down onto me in a sticky, pearly torrent. At this very moment I cum as well, crying out as a massive load ejects from the head of my dick and lands back onto my own body, mixing with the unicorn's spunk to form a beautiful swirling cocktail.

The crowd goes wild, absolutely beside themselves with enthusiasm as I climb to my feet and give a wave. As my eyes scan across the bevy of fans I spot my roommate, Bipper, his face streaked with prideful tears.

Our eyes lock and I give him a nod, the two of us thankful for the incredible direction that our lives have suddenly taken tonight, and the incredible direction that America will be taking in the future.

Bernie holds my hand in his hoof and hoists it up into the air. "I want you all to meet my new vice president!" the creature announces. "Now, he may not have the best political chops, but he's the best lover I have ever had and, with your support, I think he's going to be the best lover for America!"

A smile creeps across my face, filled with absolute warmth and happiness. We've got a long road ahead of us, but it's a road that I'm ready to travel with this handsome unicorn by my side.

PRESIDENT DOMALD LOCH NESS TROMP POUNDS AMERICA'S BUTT

One thing that I've always had going for me is my confidence as a journalist, not that it was always deserved. Looking back, much of my gusto over the last year has been youthful ignorance, a feeling that I can really make a difference out here reporting for the American public.

Over time, however, I've found myself beaten down by this whole process. However, by no means am I one of the grizzled, bitter old journalists that surround me as we board the massive 757. These men and women have lost everything, a blank soulless expression behind their eyes as they dream of the life that they could have had. I'm not there yet, but it's coming.

It's only been a year but, of all the years to start, this is the one that is most likely to drive you up a wall and break your spirit; election season.

By nature, all politicians lie; it's essentially in their job description. Some folks obviously lie more than others, but regardless of who's running for office, you're going to have quite a bit of fluff to sort through if you want to find anything tangible. Of course, when something does happen to slip through the cracks it can explode in a wave of tabloid-level excitement. A simple gaff from some presidential candidate can completely shift the political landscape overnight.

This is why my subject this week is such an anomaly; he seems to be immune to gaffs. Things that other politicians would have, traditionally, gotten burned at the stake for, he can throw out with a smile and receive tremendous support from across the Republican base. They are eating up every word of it, and it would appear that this candidate has developed a real shot at a seat in The White House.

The reason why this is all working out so well for him is actually not as illusive as it might seem, although it goes in direct contradiction to something that I just said. For the first time, a politician seems to be honestly speaking his mind on the issues, throwing the typical presidential campaign playbook to the side and simply speaking from his heart.

Unfortunately, that heart seems to be a little misguided.

"Welcome aboard Tromp Air," says an attractive young woman as I reach the top of the stairs that lead to the door of this beautiful plane, "we look forward to spending the week with you."

I give her a smile and a nod and then step inside, walking down a short hallway that opens up into several rows of seats for fellow members of the press. I recognize a some familiar faces and throw out a few waves, choosing to snag a spot next to my friend ' from Milk Magazine.

We shake hands.

"So what's old Milk Magazine want from Domald Tromp?" I ask him.

Barno shrugs, "Typical feature about the guy's favorite chocolate milk brand, ask him what he thinks of strawberry milk; fat free, two percent. Just the usual. You still with Bowling Bones?"

I nod, unable to keep a smile from creeping across my face. I may be starting to get jaded but I still can't believe that I actually write for the legendary Bowling Bones magazine, the leading counter-culture voice for generations.

Barno notices my expression. "Don't lose that, kid," he tells me. "That enthusiasm is going to keep you young."

Barno has been doing this for eight years now, so I respect his advice.

"I'm not that young," I offer. "Twenty-two."

Barno just shakes his head and laughs, "Good god, don't even talk to me about young and old, kid. You have no idea what you're talking about."

Suddenly, the loudspeaker above us chimes in, interrupting our conversation. "Alright, if everyone could have a seat we're about to take off," says the voice. "Go ahead and turn off your phones and then you can reconnect to our inflight wifi once we reach cruising altitude."

Me, Barno and the rest of the press corps do as we're told, powering off our electronic devices for a shockingly calming moment of real human interaction with one another.

Suddenly, everyone is chatting pleasantly, living their lives outside of their little black screens for a brief moment of bliss. A strange wave of relief washed over me as I lean back into my chair and let the inertia of the plane overwhelm my senses. The vehicle begins to tremble and roar, eventually lifting off and cruising up towards the clouds above. Soon we will be in Iowa, the week's first official campaign stop.

Eventually, the captain returns over the intercom to inform us that we've reached cruising altitude and we are free to turn everything on once again. The cabin erupts in a series of bleeps and bloops as phones, laptops and printers start to power on. The chaos of life on the campaign trail returns.

Suddenly, there is movement at the head of the press cabin as billionaire Domald Tromp emerges with a wide smile.

The man is slightly pudgy and his golden comb-over hair is awkward as hell, but he does have some sort of strange charm to him that I can't quite put my finger on. There's also something else, something lurking just beneath the surface of the presidential hopeful's confident presence that seems weirdly off, almost inhuman, in a way.

"Hi everybody!" says Tromp with a wave. "Welcome aboard, I just wanted to come out here and say that I'm so glad to have you here with me, so glad. I cannot even tell you how nice it is to be up in the clouds with you guys and not those losers down below, am I right?"

The collection of journalists nods awkwardly.

"You know, I'm running for president but the president's plane is actually smaller than this, by quite a lot. Did you know this?" Domald Tromp asks.

Again, his remarks are met with a strange smattering of cautious affirmation.

"We're raffling out positions over the week for one-on-one interviews," Tromp explains. "Not all of you are going to get a chance to talk with me but, what can I say, I'm a busy man. Just like with the immigration issues in this country, we don't have time to wait around and see what happens, am I right?"

"Speaking of immigration, I was wondering if you had anything you'd like to say about the dinosaurs who are upset about your racist comments regarding them crossing the border into America," Barno suddenly interjects.

I glance over at my friend, admiring his old school journalistic instincts. The guy saw an opportunity and he took it, a real pit bull.

"Well, first of all I was talking about illegal dinosaurs, not legal dinosaurs," Tromp explains. "If you were paying attention you'd know that, but you know what? I think you're kind of a third-rate journalist for asking that question. That's what I think."

The entire room is stunned into silence by this comment, reeling from the fact that this politician has somehow already turned the tables on them. While the press corps once held the keys to the castle, it appears that Domald Tromp is content on simply bashing the gate in with a battering ram.

"I was just asking if you'd like to clarify," explains Barno, clearly taken off guard by the aggression that has suddenly been directed his way.

"You know, I've been running a billion dollar company from a long time now and we've been very successful, very successful. A lot of people ask me the key to my success and you know what I tell them? I tell that that I surround myself with great, great people. I avoid the clowns and, you know what I think?" Tromp asks, nodding towards Barno.

"What?" Barno replies, his voice shaking a little.

"I have to be honest with you, I think you're kind of a clown," Domald Tromps says. "Barno, you're fired."

The next thing I know, two of the stewardesses are rushing down the hallway and unbuckling my friend from his seat. Barno seems utterly confused but he goes along with it, allowing the women to roughly carry him down the aisle by either arm as the rest of us look on in horror. Moments later, the door of the plane springs open and the entire cabin is flooded with a rush of cool air the sends papers flying.

Immediately, Barno starts to struggle against the stewardesses, but it is already too late. There is a wild yell as my friend is thrown from the airplane, whipping out into the vast blue sky and then plummeting down through the clouds behind us as he tumbles end over end.

The door slams shut, leaving the room in total silence.

"That's what I think of lightweight journalist. I think that's fair," says Domald Tromp.

Seconds later, one of the candidate's aids comes over and whispers something into Tromps ear. Domald nods in understanding and then raises his hand towards us.

"Alright, I have some preparing to do for my speech in Iowa tonight, it was great to meet you all," Tromp says enthusiastically, then returns to the other end of the plane.

That night in Iowa, the crowd is absolutely buzzing with excitement. Around me is a fairly broad collection of people, but not a single unicorn, bigfoot or dinosaur.

We are in an old airplane hanger, a stage erected at one end of the vast space while giant American flag banners hang throughout. The stage lights are dim, ready and waiting for the master of ceremonies to appear and give this crowd want they want, a way to vent their overwhelming anger towards the current political climate. There is a lot of rage in this room tonight, but it shows itself in many different ways.

I did a few interviews with Tromp supporters on the way in and learned a lot about the thinking that goes into someone's desire to vote for this madman. As I said before, these people are angry with the way the country is going, and rightfully so, but they are also afraid. With the economy in the state that it's in there is nothing more terrifying for these folks than losing their jobs, and with more and more dinosaurs crossing over the border every day, that type of blue collar security is getting harder and harder to come by.

Suddenly, the crowd around me erupts in a raucous cheer as the man himself, Domald Tromps, walks out onto the stage. Once more, I find there to be something incredibly strange about his walk, a sort of hop that just doesn't quite match with the rest of his billionaire demeanor.

"Thank you, Iowa!" shouts Tromp into the microphone before him. "It's great to be here!"

That's all it takes for the presidential hopeful to receive a second burst of wild applause, the crowd's roar growing to an absolutely deafening volume around me.

Eventually, Domald raises his hand and then lowers it slowly, signaling the group that he is read to speak once more. I immediately pull out my notepad and start writing down ideas for the article, completely inspired by the way that Tromp has is audience completely enraptured with him. It's incredible, like some kind of strange religious experience.

I notice now that many of the people around me have started to cry, their eyes running over with salty streams of tears and makeup that streak haphazardly down their cheeks. This is not just a case of the sniffles; these people are full-on bawling their eyes out in the presence of Mr. Tromp.

"I look around and all I see are winners here tonight," Tromp says. "When I become president, you would not believe how much winning there is going to be. We are going to win on the economy, we are going to win on freedom, we are going to win on immigration."

From out of the loudspeaker's positioned around the room there is suddenly an eruption of sound, a bald eagle screeching followed closely by a short but, admittedly, ripping guitar solo.

The audience loses it in the same way that I've now come to expect, and through the chaos I begin to now hear the a handful of words.

"Get those one horns out of our country!" a man says with a thick southern accent.

"Round 'em up and kill 'em!" an older woman chimes in. "Shoot 'em in the head and say you're fired!"

Suddenly, all of the fascination that I'd had with this situation is overwhelmed by something else, something powerful and heavy that floods my soul and sends a sharp chill down my spine; fear.

What was once something of a joke about the political climate and an absurdist commentary on celebrity culture has suddenly evolved, becoming all too real.

"When I'm president, everyone will get a nice, juicy, delicious steak dinner!" Tromp promises. "Every single one of you will get that, you think I'm lying? Listen, I can accord it, I've run billion dollar companies and I know what I'm talking about. I can afford a steak dinner for every American citizen because I think that's what America really wants. Am I right?"

I suddenly feel my phone start to vibrate within my pocket. I pull it out and glance down, noticing the number for Barno's boss, the editor of Milk Magazine.

Quickly, I make my way back through the crowd and out of the hanger, which is surrounded by a wide-open field of corn stalks that seems to stretch on endlessly around me.

I answer. "Hello, this is Pibbles for Bowling Bone Magazine."

"Pibbles," comes a deep, commanding voice. "It's Lon Bisk, I need to know if I can trust you."

"You can trust me," I say, taking a few steps out into the cornfield, even farther from the earshot of any unsavory characters.

"Are you aware that Barno Yawn-Starman was murdered earlier today?" Lon asks.

"I witnessed it," I tell him.

"Then you know that Domald Tromp is out of control," Lon says. "You know that he's willing to do whatever it takes to become president and he's not going to stop until he gets there."

"People love him," I say. "They're angry and he's channeling it."

"What if I told you that I had some dirt on Domald Tromp that could change everything?" the man asks.

I laugh. "Then I'd tell you that you're kidding yourself," I reply. "The guy just murdered someone today and his poll numbers went through the roof. American's loved it."

"This is bigger than throwing Barno out of a plane," assures Lon, "this could blow the lid off of everything."

I immediately recognize the deep seriousness of Lon's voice. This scoop is the real deal.

"I'm listening," I tell the man.

"Don't listen… look," explains Lon. "I'm going to be emailing you something in the next hour."

"In an hour, I'll be back on Tromp's plane," I counter.

"You have wifi up there, right?" Lon asks. "On the plane?"

"Sure do," I tell him.

"Then get ready for quite the flight."

By the time we leave Iowa for New Hampshire it's well past midnight, and most of the others around me are sleeping soundly in their seats. I'm somehow both exhausted and completely wired after today, my body drained but the thought of resting absolutely ridiculous.

Instead, I sit wide-awake in the dark cabin, refreshing my email every few minutes while I wait for the arrival of Lon's smoking gun.

I can't help but think, why me? Of all the people that the editor of Milk Magazine has in his Rolodex, why would he pick me to unload this massive scoop?

Maybe he needed something broader to make sure it was taken seriously, I think. Sometimes the milk readership has a hard time with that.

Suddenly, a loud, electronic ding interrupts my thoughts. I glance down and see an unopened message sitting there in my mailbox, just waiting to reveal its secrets. Without hesitation, I open the email and find it blank, a single attachment included.

I open the attachment.

Immediately, my computer screen is filled with a large, scanned document. It takes me a moment to realize exactly what this is and when I do I gasp suddenly, nearly jumping right out of my seat. Suddenly, it all makes sense.

I glance back and forth over my shoulder to see if anyone else is watching, and then lean in towards my screen to get a better look. Sure enough, the image is exactly what I thought; a birth certificate. Not just any birth certificate, but one that was presented in Scotland on the year of Domald's birth. Tromp wasn't born in the United States.

Not only that, but the birth certificate clearly reveals that the candidates full name is Domald Loch Ness Tromp.

Suddenly, it all makes sense; the strange way that Domald moves, the green color of his skin, the long neck. Domald Tromp is the Loch Ness Monster.

Not only is this shocking in its own right, but for one other, powerfully hypocritical reason, the Loch Ness Monster is a plesiosaur. In other words, Domald Tromps is secretly one of the dinosaurs he so vehemently hates.

I've just finished piecing all of this together when suddenly one of the stewardesses appears in the doorway before me.

"Mr. Pibbles Pooch," she says, addressing me quietly. "Your raffle number as been called to interview Mr. Tromp."

I glance around in confusion. "Right now?" I ask.

The stewardess nods. "Yes, sir. Please come with me."

I close my laptop and reluctantly stand, my heart now beating hard in my chest as the woman leads me away from my peers and down the lavish hallway of this luxurious 757.

This is the first time I have been down to the far end of the aircraft, and I have to admit that, despite my overwhelming fear, I am truly amazed at just how lavish this vehicle really is. No expense has been spared; every gold plated detail installed with the finest attention to detail.

Eventually, we reach Tromps large office and the stewardess opens the door for me, closing it quickly after I step inside.

"Mr. Pibbles," Domald Tromp says with a smile. He motions for me to sit down across the desk from him, with what I now realize is a dark green flipper.

How could I not have noticed this before? Tromp is so clearly the Loch Ness Monster that I can't even imagine seeing him any other way.

I have a seat across the desk from Tromp, taking in the spectacular glory of his incredible aerial office. To my right is a waterfall, complete with large koi fish and a blue heron that has somehow been trained to live in harmony with them. To my right is a giant window looking out across the clouds below us and the starlit sky above.

"I suppose you've got a lot of question for me," Domald Tromp says, "but before we begin, I've got just one question for you."

I try my best to remain calm, although I am certain that my anxiety is showing through at this point. My breathing has grown heavy and sweat begins to form in beads across my forehead.

"My question is; what are you planning on doing with that birth certificate?" Domald asks.

I freeze, my brain struggling to find any reasonable response that it can and coming up completely empty.

"Cat got your tongue?" Tromp snarls.

"What birth certificate?" I finally ask.

"The one in your email," the prehistoric creature replies, smugly.

I realize now that I have been caught red-handed, and straight-up denial will get me absolutely nowhere.

"How did you know?" I ask. "Are you monitoring all of the computers on this network? You know that is illegal, right?"

"Do you think I care?" Domald asks.

I let out a long sigh, completely certain of the answer. "No."

"No," the Loch Ness Monster confirms, shaking his head, "of course I don't care, Mr. Pooch. Desperate times call for desperate measures."

"So what are you going to do with me?" I ask him, my voice trembling. "Throw me out of the plane like you did to my friend Barno?"

The aquatic billionaire just stares at me blankly. He is impossible to get a read on, his emotions drifting carefully just below the surface of his green, scaly face.

Eventually, the dinosaur stands up and, without a word, begins to make his way around the desk towards me. I gaze up, trembling in fear as the beast approaches, terrified by the thought of whatever might happen next.

"You know, the smart thing for me to do would be to fire you," says Domald.

"But, I don't work for you," I counter.

"Listen to me," the monster says, ignoring my statement. "I'm saying it would be the smart thing to do, but I'm not gonna do it. You know why? Because I like you. You're a killer, Pibbles, a real killer."

"Thank you," I say with a slight nod and a gulp.

Tromp takes a seat at the edge of his desk and eyes me up and down, looking me over with his massive Loch Ness pupils.

"You're not a clown like the rest," the creature says, placing a flipper on my knee.

As we touch for the first time I can't help but flinch, incredibly uncomfortable with our physical connection, but as the seconds pass I can slowly feel myself relaxing, adjusting to the prehistoric candidate's presence. Eventually, I feel the tingle of something strange and erotic pulsing deep within me, an ache for something more as the monster begins to run his flipper up and down my leg.

"What is this?" I ask.

"I'm gonna tell it like it is," the creature explains, "because that's just the way I do things. I love America, I really do. In fact, I love America so much that I want to pound it in the butt."

"In the butt?" I ask.

"Yes," Domald nods, "and if I'm going to start the process of pounding America in the butt, I'd like to start with you. With your beautiful, muscular rump."

I'm about to protest and pull away when suddenly I realize that, in truth, I don't really want to. I said at the beginning that there was something strangely intoxicating about Domald Tromp, and I've only just not realized what it is; an extreme, gay lust.

"I've never been with another man," I finally tell him, my voice trembling. "I'm straight."

"So am I," says Domald softly, "but I'm not another man. I'm the Loch Ness Monster."

The creature leans in and kisses me hard on the lips, prompting me to pull back slightly, but then slowly give in to the sensation of Domald's incredible touch. I suddenly find myself overwhelmed with arousal for this brazen, golden haired politician.

Suddenly overwhelmed with ecstasy, I push back my chair and slip down onto the floor in front of him, looking up at the creature before me with a playful grin. Being that he is the Loch Ness Monster, Domald wears no pants, so it is clear to see that his massive cock is growing thicker and fuller by the minute. Soon enough, Tromps erection is standing at full attention before me, jutting out at my face like a deep green Popsicle.

Without hesitation, I open up and swallow the reptile politician deep, pushing down as far as I can onto the candidate's presidential dick.

Domald lets out a long, satisfied moan, placing his flippers on the back of my head and driving me lower and lower until suddenly I push up against my gag reflex and retch loudly. Suddenly I pull back, gasping and sputtering for air as spit hands limply between my lips and the head of Tromp's massive shaft.

"I'm not some loser clown," I assure The Domald, "one more try."

I open my mouth and take him again, pushing down slowly and trying my best to relax as his rod sinks deeper and deeper. It's not long before his length is teasing up against the edge of my gag reflex for another attempt, only this time I'm ready for him, allowing his giant cock to slip past in a stunning deep throat.

Now Domald Tromp's dick sits fully within me, consumed to the hilt as his beautiful balls hang against my chin. Their size is impressive, revealing the creature to be a real man's man, despite not being a man at all.

After holding the beast here for a while I finally run out of air and pull back, then immediately get to work bobbing my head up and down across his large shaft. I move slowly and deliberately at first and then eventually start to gain speed, pumping my tight lips across his length with a frantic enthusiasm I never quite knew that I possessed.

The dinosaur is utterly beside himself with pleasure, moaning and groaning and slapping his long scaly tail against the floor of the office.

Eventually, though, Domald has had enough of my mouth, craving something much more explicit from my muscular body.

"Come on," Tromp says, reaching out a flipper and lifting me up to my feet. The next thing I know, the dinosaur is directing me over to the massive window before us, pushing me up against the glass and pulling down my pants with his powerful flippers.

I glance back at him with an excited smile as the large dinosaur climbs into position behind me, aligning the head of his massive shaft with the hole of my tightly puckered asshole.

"I am a one man weapon of change!" the creature declares. "I pledge to pound the butt of every willing American across this beautiful land, starting tonight!"

"This is truly historic," I tell the presidential hopeful. "It's an honor."

The dinosaur immediately thrusts forward and I let out a loud yelp, my body trying its best to adjust to the incredible sensation of fullness that overwhelms me. I brace myself against the window, trying to will my body to relax as the creature behind me begins with his slow, firm thrusts.

The clouds have cleared and below us I can now see a massive sea of city lights stretching out for what seems like forever.

"Do you see that?" Domald asks, picking up speed with his powerful thrusts up my asshole. "Do you see that fucking city down there?"

"I see it," I confirm, my body trembling with pleasure as the dinosaur plows into me. I reach down and grab ahold of my rock hard dick, beating myself off to the rhythm of Tromp's hammering from behind.

"I own all of that," Domald Tromp groans erotically, losing control of himself in a fit of lustful emotion "all of it!"

"That's so fucking hot!" I scream. "Pound me harder, Mr. Tromp!"

Now the Loch Ness Monster is slamming into me as hard as he can, his massive cock working like a jackhammer within the depths of my tight anus. I am beside myself with pleasure, the first beautiful sparks of prostate orgasm blossoming within me.

There is something incredible about being taken by such a strong, patriotic beast, even if he is really from Scotland. There is a passion within Domald that lurks behind every movement, every look, and every anal plow. He has completely overpowered me, and I'm loving every second of it.

Eventually, Domald Trumps tires of impressing me with his obscene amount of real estate and pulls us back away from the window, spinning me around and then laying me across the desk with my legs spread wide. The Jurassic billionaire places his dick at the entrance of my reamed out asshole and slams forward, immediately getting to work within me while I beat of my cock in a delirious gay trance.

"Fuck me!" I scream, "Fuck me President Loch Ness Tromp! Pound my ass like you'll pound the ass of all Americans!"

I can tell by the creature's pace that he is now growing close blowing his load, and I follow just behind. I can feel my body start to tense up and then break into a wild spasm of uncontrollable bliss, my legs shaking frantically in the air.

"Cum up my tight gay ass!" I scream, just as I eject my load.

The jizz flies through the air, splattering across my muscular chest in a beautiful Pollack pattern that swirls over my tan skin.

Suddenly, the Loch Ness Monster is cumming, as well, pushing deep within me and holding tight as he lets out a tremendous roar that is reserved for only the most incredible political titans. It shakes the entire desk, and the plane around us, a vocalization of this candidate's extreme love for the United States of America.

I can feel his spunk filling my asshole to the brim, giggling as it eventually squirts out from the sides of my tightly packed rectum and then drips onto the desk below it.

"Fuck," Domald Tromp finally says, pulling out of me and spilling his seed everywhere in a glorious mess. "That was great."

"You're just what this country needs," I tell the monster.

It turns out that alienating the entire dinosaur demographic is not the best political strategy, and when election night rolls around Domald Loch Ness Tromp loses by a landslide.

Despite our brief and important moment together on the campaign trail, I never saw the creature again, but I also never revealed his secret. I'd like to think that we came to some kind of understanding up there above the clouds, a lover's pact that would forever remain unbroken.

However, that doesn't mean that Lon from Milk Magazine shared the same bond that I did with Mr. Tromp. Soon enough, Milk blew the lid off of everything, sending his publication into the stratosphere and sending Domald Tromp slinking back down into the depths of Loch Ness from which he came.

Some say that, on cold dark nights, you can hear his voice still drifting faintly across the Scottish lake, moaning into the harsh winds. You have to listen very carefully, but if you're lucky you can hear it.

"You're fired," the creature bellows out to the world that turned its back on him.

SLAMMED IN THE BUTT BY DOMALD TROMP'S ATTEMPT TO AVOID ACCUSATIONS OF PLAGIARISM BY REMOVING ALL FACTS OR CONCRETE PLANS FROM HIS REPUBLICAN NATIONAL CONVENTION SPEECH

I've been a speech writer for a long time, and never before have I felt this kind of pressure to create something spectacular, something moving, and most importantly, something original.

When I tell my friends this, they say that I'm putting way too much pressure on myself, that it really doesn't matter because Domald Tromp could say anything and the conservative crowds would still be swooning over him in droves. I'll admit, they're not wrong, the man has been spouting off racist and sexist remarks any chance that he gets, and he literally threw a reporter out of a plane on the campaign trail earlier this year.

Neither of these things amounted to any kind of substantial negative press, and the latter one was actually spun into an example of him being a take charge candidate who would do anything for his country.

The thing is, even though I probably *could* turn in a sheet of incomprehensible syllables, I take a certain amount of pride in my work, and I want this speech to be good.

You're probably wondering the same thing that everyone always wonders when they first meet me, if I know that Tromp is such a horrible person then why am I still writing for him? Why am I participating in a campaign that many people believe is going to lead to the wholesale destruction of America?

I'm going to be honest; if I could write for one of the other candidates, I would. Unfortunately, this is the job that I have and it's a hell of a position, one that is right on track with wiping out my student loans and helping me prepare for the future. I need this job, but when it comes time to vote I will definitely not be pulling the lever for Tromp.

This week it's the Republican National Convention, a time when all of the eyes of the country will be on the Republican Party as they officially announce their nominee for president, which is certain to be Mr. Tromp at this point. There are a lot of speeches to be planned, as the convention features wall-to-wall speakers on almost every issue imaginable.

Tonight, most of the campaign staff has gathered in a luxurious back room in the deepest parts of the convention arena, surrounding a large flat screen television with a live feed of the evening's festivities. It's the end of the first night and we are anxiously awaiting the on stage arrival of Domald's First Lady, Morlinda Tromp.

Everyone is anxious, although these feelings of tension aren't typical for the situation at hand. Normally, one of us in the speech-writing department is the only one on edge, waiting to see if their words hit the mark or miss it completely and result in a swift firing from The Domald himself. Tonight, however, we know that our positions are secure and yet we are more nervous than ever.

This is because Morlinda Tromp has decided to write tonight's speech herself.

Typically, this would be flatly shot down the second that it was suggested, but Domald Tromp is not a typical candidate and this is not a typical campaign. Despite a hefty amount of protesting from those of us behind the scenes, Morlinda is going to be speaking her own words tonight, and we have no idea what's going to happen.

On screen, the crowd erupts into a raucous applause, bursting to their feet as the potential next first lady of the United States walks out onto the stage. She appears confident and powerful, radiating with the prowess of a seasoned politician even though English isn't even her first language. This is a very, very good way to start things off.

"Hello! Thank you, thank you!" Morlinda begins. Everyone here on the staff is watching with rapt attention, our hearts slamming hard within our chests as we await her self-written words.

The potential next first lady pauses for a moment, soaking up the affection and love from the Republican Convention around her. Finally, she continues. "The Democrats don't see the danger in what they are doing here," Morlinda announces. "Genetic power is the most awesome force that earth has ever seen and the Democrats are wielding it like a kid who has just found his dad's gun."

Immediately, my breath catches in my throat. It appears the Morlinda has a point here, but the way that she is expressing that point is nothing short of bizarre. I have no idea where she could possibly be heading with this and I bristle at the mentions of genetics and irresponsible gun use. I glance around the room and see that other members of the staff are getting nervous as well.

"I'll tell you the problem with the scientific power that the Democrats are using!" Morlinda says, throwing her hands in the air in a confident gesture. "It didn't require any discipline to attain it. They've read what others have done and then they took the next step. They stood on the shoulders of giants to accomplish something fast and easy, and before they knew what they had they've packaged it and slapped it on a lunchbox and now they are selling it!"

It's clear now that all of us are behind the scenes are in panic mode, utterly confused about where she is headed with this. Someone can't help but ask loudly, "What the hell is she talking about?"

I wish I knew but, at this point, I'm beginning to get the strange sense that I've heard these words before. I have no idea where, or when, but there is something utterly familiar about this rather bizarre diatribe.

Morlinda is screaming now, her eyes wild with patriotic enthusiasm. "The Democrats have spent so much time trying to figure out if they could, they never stopped to think about if they should! Thank you!"

The crowd is on their feet now, cheering in a frantic standing ovation as Morlinda waves and turns away from the podium, seemingly confident in a job well done.

I'm not as happy as she is. In fact, I'm downright horrified.

"Oh my god," I say aloud, suddenly realizing where I've heard all of these words before. "Oh my fucking god."

"Oh come on, it was weird, but it wasn't *that* bad," one of the other writers says to me, putting his hand on my shoulder.

I shake my head. "No, this is *really* bad. Don't you realize what that was?"

I suddenly realize that I've got the attention of the entire room, the crew standing in complete silence as all eyes come to rest on me.

"That was just Bein Balcom's speech from the movie Jurassic Mark!" I exclaim. "You know, when they're having dinner and they've learned about the dinosaurs that Mark hired for his new theme park?"

I watch as the others quickly start looking up phrases from the speech on their phones, gasping in astonishment when they realize I am right. Suddenly, their phones start ringing and, soon enough, the entire room has devolved into crisis mode, the press division struggling to put out fires left and right.

"Mr. Tromp will see you now," offers his assistant, strolling assertively into the hotel lobby where I've been patiently seated for the last hour.

Normally, I have much quicker access to the man who I'm speech writing for, but the last few days have been absolutely insane. The controversy generated from Morlinda's plagiarized speech has done nothing but blossom into a talking point that the campaign cannot seem to get rid of no matter how hard we try, and it has put me into the exact position that I did not want to find myself in.

While I had once been quiet relaxed about Domald Tromp's upcoming speech, I now find the eyes of the world are glued onto me and my words, whether they know it yet or not.

I stand up and follow the assistant to the elevator, where we soon ascend to the top floor penthouse of this beautiful hotel nestled right across the street from the convention arena.

"You know, Senator Ted Cobs refused to endorse Tromp at the convention last night," the assistant tells me.

I'm not sure what is gained from making this comment, other than stressing me out even more, so I just nod in response.

"This speech better be good," the assistant continues.

We finally reach the top floor and the elevator door slides open, revealing a massive boardroom covered in luxurious golden trappings. There is a long white marble table that runs down the length of the chamber, and at the end sits Tromp himself.

"Perper, have a seat!" Mr. Tromp offers with the wave of his hand.

He's so far away that I can barely see him, but I do as he asks, taking a seat in a lavish chair that's been positioned at the end.

"Do you like this table? I think this is just the best table," Tromp says. "We had it brought in for this meeting."

"Yeah, it's nice," I assure him.

There is an awkward moment of silence between us as I wait for the rather intimidating candidate to continue.

Finally, Tromp speaks. "I'm sure you know that tonight is very important for us," he says. "I just wanted to make sure you knew that. After Morlinda's speech, we need something fresh and powerful. Now, I know you're the best speechwriter out there, and I believe in you, Perper, I really do… but you've gotta knock this one out of the park."

"Yes sir, I think I've got something really good for you cooked up," I tell him.

"Good?" Tromp asks.

"I'm sorry," I correct myself. "Great."

"That's more like it," says Tromp.

"I've got the speech right here," I tell him, holding up a manila folder. I start to stand so that I can walk over and hand it to him but Tromp stops me in my tracks.

"Just leave it there when you go," says the candidate.

"Okay," I reply, trying my best not to be awkward during this *extremely awkward* exchange.

"There's nothing weird in it, is there?" asks Tromp. "Anything that the Democrats can pick apart and turn into a… viral sensation?"

"I don't think so," I tell him. "I mean, no, sir."

"Good, good," offers Tromp. "What about… facts? Are there any of those?"

"Facts?" I question. "You don't want facts?"

Domald sighs loudly. "Listen, we've got a lot of accusations of plagiarism flying around lately. The campaign has decided that it's not a good idea to have any concrete plans or facts in this speech, as that could appear to be lifted from somewhere else. Really, we need the whole thing to just be completely empty on the inside."

"Fluff?" I question.

"Feel good stuff," Domald clarifies. "Basically, just throw togeather a bunch of words that seem patriotic, arranged in a way that barely makes any sense so that you can't really pin down what I'm trying to say. Maybe try adding 'believe me' after a bunch of lines, something like that just to bulk it up a bit. I'm trying to go for the longest convention speech of all time to assert my dominance."

"I... I don't know what to tell you," I stammer. "There are facts and plans in the speech that I wrote, at least, as much as I could gather." I stop there, not wanting to admit how hard of a time I'd had trying to come up with any sort of concrete message from the campaign regardless.

"That's no good," Domald says. The businessman reaches over and presses a button on his desk intercom.

"Robobba," he barks. "Get in here with some coffee for Perper, he needs to rewrite this speech and remove anything that makes sense."

"Right away, sir," comes the voice on the other end.

At this very moment, I can feel my heart break, understanding that I have no other choice but accept Domald's wishes. Unless I want to get fired, it's too late to turn back now.

It's late when the knock comes hard against my hotel room door. I was fast asleep, finally succumbing to the warm embrace of my bed after tossing and turning for hours. Sure, the speech had gone over well with the people at the convention, but as someone with a more critical outlook myself, I couldn't help feeling guilty about what I had done. There was absolutely nothing concrete put forward in the statement that had been read tonight, just an abstract pile of American imagery that will, hopefully, make little enough sense to avoid a plagiarism accusation.

"Hello?" I call out, looking over at my clock and seeing that it's midnight. I reach over and turn on the bedside lamp.

"Is this Perper Tunk's room?" calls a deep voice from the hallway outside.

I'm not sure if I should answer, but finally my curiosity gets the best of me. "Yeah, this is Perper," I reply. "Who's asking?"

"Your speech!" the voice calls back.

This is the last response that I was expecting, and I find myself completely dumbfounded. "What do you mean?" I question.

"I'm your speech, the one that you wrote for Tromp," the voice continues. "It's late, and I wasn't sure where to go."

I finally stand up and walk over to the door, pulling back the chain lock and then cracking it open. To my surprise, I find the physical manifestation of Domald Tromp's Republican National Convention speech standing before me in all of his swirling, fear mongering glory. The speech is handsome as hell, and as the one who crafted him I take quite a bit of pride in saying this. I'm not gay, but if I was I can't deny that I'd probably find myself a little turned on by his midnight arrival.

"What's wrong?" I ask. "You don't have a place to stay tonight?"

The sentient speech shakes his head. "You didn't give me one when you wrote me, you didn't give me anything," he explains.

A surge of guilt suddenly pulses through me. He's right, after all. While my first draft of the speech had been concrete and multifaceted, this version is just a pretty face, gorgeous and triumphant on the outside but completely lacking any substance.

"You can't go stay with the Tromps?" I question.

"They don't want anything to do with me," explains the living manifestation of my own political rhetoric. "I just gained sentience today, so I'm not technically a citizen. Tromp calls me an illegal. He hates me; says I'm a criminal."

I let out a long sigh. This is all my fault, and now this soulless but well meaning speech is my responsibility. "Alright, you can come in," I say, opening the door. "What's your name?"

"Sherpo." The speech looks past me at my rather nice hotel room, his eyes coming to rest on the single king bed. "There's only one bed," he observes.

As I mentioned before, I'm not gay, but I'd be lying if I didn't admit that the way Sherpo makes note of this sends a sharp chill down my spine.

The handsome living presidential nomination acceptance speech steps inside and my heart starts to race even faster, realizing just how muscular the sentient collection of words truly is. I was told to make him easy on the eyes, and that's exactly what I did.

As the speech walks past me our hands brush and suddenly both of us have stopped dead in our tracks, our eyes locking in a strange moment of heated tension. Neither of us dares make a move, but we're both thinking exactly the same thing.

"I made you... very well," I say, the words leaving my lips with an almost involuntary ease.

"You did," the speech says with a smile. He hesitates for a moment and then finally continues. "I may be empty and full of factually dubious fluff, but there's not denying that there's a connection between us."

He's right. I want this sentient collection of conservative political pandering, and I want him now. I close the door behind us.

"What are you doing?" asks Sherpo.

Suddenly consumed by arousal, I drop to my knees before the handsome speech, grabbing ahold of his thickening rod and beating him off with an enthusiasm that surprises even myself.

The sentient arrangement of words looks down at me warmly, as if he'd been expecting this. "You like that dick?" he questions playfully, making it painfully clear that he's well aware of his own devious charm.

"It's amazing," I offer, "I had no idea that I could be so attracted to the physical manifestation of my own political rhetoric."

"Believe it," the speech says confidently.

His swagger is alluring beyond belief, drowning my better judgment even more in wave after wave of lustful attraction. I am falling for Sherpo, and falling for him hard.

After a good while of stroking, I open wide and take the speech's massive cock into my mouth, wrapping my lips tightly around him as I begin to pump my head up and down across his length. His cock is big enough that it's honestly quite a struggle to get down, but I do my best to service him. My lips are stretched tight, barely able to contain his girth.

After a good while of modestly sucking him off like this I finally go for it and push my face all the way down onto the full enormity of his rod, somehow relaxing the muscles in my neck and taking Sherpo in an incredible deep throat. Having never participated in a gay experience before, I'm shocked by my own sexual prowess, savoring every moment as I gaze up at the speech with my head fully impaled across his shaft.

The living statement holds me here for a while, placing his hands against the back of my head and waiting until I've just about ran out of air before he lets me up. I erupt in a frantic gasp, sputtering as I try to collect myself and reeling from the newfound gay lust that courses through my system.

"I want you to pound me," I tell Sherpo frantically. "I want you to slam my butthole right here on this hotel bed."

"Gladly," the speech accepts with alluring confidence.

behind his expression.

"What is it?" I question.

"I know that you love me," the sentient political message says, "I was written to be loved, but it's all surface level. You don't have to pretend with me, I know there's no real meaning."

He's right, and I know it.

"It's okay," the speech assures me, standing up and heading for the door.

"Wait!" I call out, causing Sherpo to stop in his tracks.

The conservative political statement turns around and looks back at me, revealing the pain in his eyes.

"You might be completely inaccurate, and you might be deeply pandering," I offer, "but you're *my* pandering speech, and if someone out there is going to take care of you it might as well be me."

"You really mean that?" the sentient collection of words asks.

I nod. "Of course I do. I wrote you, you're my responsibility now. Maybe instead of fucking over America, you can just start fucking over me." I give Sherpo a playful wink and he smiles in return.

"I love you," my handsome speech tells me.

"I love you, too," I say.

Unlike the words written on the living speech before me, I actually mean it.

CREAMED IN THE BUTT BY MY HANDSOME LIVING CORN

It's rare that you think of a down-home, Southern farmer in a suit and a tie, but I'm not your average farmer. Of course, there's nothing wrong with working the fields in a dirty old T-shirt and a straw hat, wiping the sweat from your brow as you till the brown soil. I can honestly say that I've put in more than enough hours doing just that.

But there are many different facets of agriculture, and as the work changes in this modern day and age, the men and women who make up our American farming industry are changing with it.

When I was younger, all that I really needed to worry about was rotating the crops and following the weather patterns, but these days it seems like every political issue under the sun has worked its way into the process of growing food.

The particular weekend's activity; crop lobbying.

While there was once a time that the veggies I planted were based on whatever I felt like growing, many large-scale farmers like me are currently being accosted by various companies who want their seeds sown.

I'll be the first to admit, getting wined and dined like this is quite the treat for a humble guy like me, and I've honestly started to really enjoy these conferences. It's just hard to look back and recognize that this is what the life of a farmer has become. I don't think I'll ever truly feel comfortable with my shirt buttoned all the way to the top and this tie wrapped around me like a noose.

"Excuse me," comes a deep, soulful voice, suddenly breaking my concentration.

I look up, my reminiscence of the good old days dissipating quickly as it's replaced by the smiling face of a large cob of corn.

"I think I'm over there," the striking corn says, pointing to the airplane seat next to me.

I should stand up and let him through, making the whole boarding process as quick and efficient as possible, but instead I just sit here and stare at him, completely taken aback by the vegetable's shockingly good looks.

"Are you alright?" the corn asks, snapping me out of it for a second time.

'Oh, yeah, sorry about that," I stammer, standing up from my seat and then stepping out into the aisle of our bustling jet as we prepare for take off. I wave my hand across the row of chairs, motioning the corn inward.

Even now, I can't take my eyes off of this muscular agricultural staple as he moves past me and then finally collapses into the window seat. He is perfectly toned from head to toe, a beautiful yellow glow shimmering off every kernel of his body.

When I take my seat once again, the vegetable introduces himself. "I'm Liplon," the corn tells me, shaking my hand.

"Matthew McConneymay," I reply, giving him a firm shake and trying my best to collect my sense. "I'm guessing you're flying to the agriculture conference, too?"

"What gave me away?" the cob of corn says with a wink.

I laugh, instantly charmed by the handsome vegetable. I can see why this corn in particular would be sent in to convince farmers of using his species in their fields; he has an overwhelming amount of charisma to go with his dashing good looks.

"You a corn man?" Matthew asks, cutting right to the chase.

I chuckle, suddenly feeling quite uncomfortable. "No, I can't say that I am."

"What are you growing?" the corn continues. "If you don't mind me asking, of course."

"Oh no, it's fine," I gush, waving his cares away as I try my best to remain as endearing as possible to the veggie. "Beets."

"Hmm," is all that Matthew says, smiling to himself, and then immediately turns to look out the window in silence.

I have to admit, this was not the response that I was expecting from a smooth talker such as this. I had been bracing myself for the hard sell, and when it doesn't happen I immediately find myself strangely disappointed.

At first I'm not sure if I should say anything, well aware that any more conversation on the matter could spark a heated debate and a sales pitch that I would, unfortunately, be forced to decline. My curiosity has gotten the best of me, though, and regardless of whether or not the corn is currently playing me like a fiddle, I need to know more.

"What?" I finally ask.

Liplon glances back at me. "I'm sorry?"

"What does hmm mean? Why should I be growing corn?"

Liplon smiles. "I mean, when's the last time you sat down and bit into a nice, juicy piece of corn? Like, really enjoyed it in a situation where your focus was entirely on the cob itself. Maybe with some salt and butter? I don't know, whatever floats your boat."

I shrug, suddenly realizing that I truly don't remember the last time this had occurred. Lately, it's been all beets at the house and, although they can certainly hit the spot of you know what you're doing, the thought of a piping hot corn on the cob really does sound fantastic at the moment.

Liplon can see the expression on my face and just laughs knowingly to himself. "See?"

"I just don't know if it makes business sense," I tell him.

The corn nods. "Yeah, I guess you're probably right."

Once more the handsome, muscular cob turns away and leaves me to simmer in my own thoughts.

The rest of the plane ride we don't say another word, each of us prepping for the long weekend of meetings and fancy business dinners ahead. Despite being the representative of such a massive food staple, the living corn next to me seems incredibly calm, as if he knows something that the rest of the world doesn't.

When we finally touch down in California and begin collecting our bags from the overhead compartment, the corn steps towards me and hands me his business card in one cool, calculated motion.

I take his card and read it aloud. "Corn."

"If you change your mind about your crops, give me a call," Liplon explains. "We'll do dinner."

"Sounds good," I confirm with a nod, but before I can look up to face him again, the vegetable is gone.

The first day of the conference is quite productive, a slew of meetings with several very persuasive foods who are glad to pay for my drinks regardless of the fact that I'm clearly not interested in switching crops any time soon. My main source of income is beets, however, and they always do a great job of showing my why this is a good relationship to maintain, taking me out for an incredible steak dinner in one of the fanciest restaurants I've ever had the good fortune to dine in. As a country boy, this is more than enough to keep me satisfied with the way things are going back home.

Still, there is something that continues to gnaw away in the back of my mind, a strange ache that throbs deep down in the darkest, gayest parts of my subconscious. What if I had a relationship with corn? My life is wonderful now, and I respect the hell out of beets, but could it be even better?

When we finish up our dinner my purple companions offer to pay for a taxi back to the hotel, but I decline, opting instead to clear my head with a nice long walk in the warm night air. The beets insist, but I'm steadfast in my decision and finally we part ways with a smile and a handshake.

It's not a far walk between our restaurant and the convention center, which is directly across from the hotel that I've been generously put up in. I'm taking my time, though, strolling leisurely as my thoughts drift this way and that.

No matter what I do, I can't stop thinking about the way the light had glistened off of the corn's beautiful rounded kernels, or even the succulent yet subtle taste that his body would create in my mouth. Suddenly, I find myself with the beginnings of a completely unexpected erection, my hardened member pushing gently against the fabric of my pants.

A farmer my entire life, this is the first time I've ever developed feelings for a food of any kind, let alone a vegetable. While the concept is a bit intimidating at first, it's actually quite comforting the longer I think about it. What would be so wrong for a farmer and his vegetable to take their relationship to the next level?

Nothing, I suddenly realize.

I reach into my pocket and pull out the card that Liplon gave me, flipping it over in my hand as my eyes scan the elegantly designed surface.

There is a phone number on the back and, seized by a moment of erotic compulsion, I call it.

I hold the phone to my ear, listening as it rings once, twice, three times. Finally, someone on the other end picks up.

"Hello?" comes the deep voice of the handsome veggie.

"Is this Liplon? The corn?" I question.

"Speaking."

It suddenly occurs to me that I have no idea what to say, no real reason for calling other than the fact that my own sexual attraction compelled me to. The silence between us is deafening, my heart kicking into double time as my brain frantically searches for something to say.

"I met you on the plane," I finally stammer.

Liplon takes his time with this information, completely chilled as he gives this space in our conversation weight.

"Matthew, right?" the corn asks.

"Yeah, that's me," I tell him, sweet relief washing over my body as Liplon remembers my name. I'd be lying if I said that I wasn't incredibly flattered.

"You thinking about switching to corn?" the golden food asks.

"I don't know," I sigh.

"Let's meet up for a drink and talk about it," Liplon offers, "where are you at?"

I glance around, finding the nearest cross street and then describing my whereabouts to the living food.

"I'll be there in two minutes," Liplon tells me, then hangs up without another word.

I'm trembling with anticipation now, fully realizing that the consequences of breaking my current beet contracts could be utterly devastating. Depending on how angry the beets got, I could lose my farm.

Of course, that's only if I break the contract, and I suddenly realize that I've done nothing so far that could get me in trouble. For the rest of the night, I'll just keep things civil. A casual drink is nothing out of the ordinary at a conference like this.

Suddenly, a beautiful yellow convertible pulls up next to me, the top down and Liplon sitting proudly in the driver's seat. He flashes a brilliant smile.

"Get in," the handsome corn on the cob commands.

All of the pent up desire that has been waiting so patiently within me suddenly explodes across my body, consumed by a frantic desire to become one with this handsome corn. Even though I am completely straight and Liplon is a male, there is no denying the energy that exchanges between us any longer.

"Whoa," I gush as we pull back from one another.

"The business can wait," Lipton tells me with a smile.

"How about some corn holing?" I offer mischievously.

Without hesitation, I turn and push the giant corn back onto the grass behind us, noticing now that an absolutely massive yellow erection has started to sprout out from his ripped body. It grows larger and larger as I begin to passionately kiss my way down his kernelled chest, drifting lower with every touch of my lips until finally my mouth is hovering directly above his swollen member.

Liplon lets out a long, powerful moan as I wrap my lips tightly around his cock. I immediately get to work moving my head up and down his length, slowly and sensually at first and then building speed. Soon enough I am bobbing my head across his length at a steady pace, allowing the corn to place his hands against the back of my skull and guide me.

"Oh fuck that feels so good, Matthew McConneymay," Liplon groans, pumping his hips back against my face.

I reach down and begin to play with his hanging yellow balls, which cases the vegetable to extenuate his pumps even more.

Finally, when I feel like things have reached an erotic peak between us, I push down as far as I can to consume his rod entirely in a expertly performed deep throat.

At least, that's what the plan was. However, things don't exactly work out that way that I expected. Greatly underestimating Liplon's size, I immediately begin to choke when his dick pushes against my gag reflex. The next thing I know I'm pulling back, releasing his shaft from my depths and retching loudly.

"You're so fucking big," I admit, struggling to regain my composure. "One more try."

I gather myself as much as possible and then attempt once more, taking the corn's dick between my lips and then slowly, confidently, lowering my head onto him. This time I am much more relaxed, and when the head of his cock reaches my gag reflex I somehow allow it to pass by without any hesitation.

Suddenly, I find myself with Liplon's giant corn dick fully inserted within my throat, his balls pressed hard against my chin.

The massive food clearly enjoys being fully consumed like this, and lets me know by throwing his head back and letting out a loud, passionate sigh of pleasure.

Within the warm confines my mouth I run my tongue across his length, up and down the shaft as I slowly begin to run out of air. This continues until, finally, I just can't take it any longer and come up sputtering and choking. A long strand of saliva hangs between the corn's dick and my hungry mouth.

"I want you to pound me," I tell him, climbing up onto the vegetable as he lies sprawled out in the grass.

I'm facing Liplon as I grab ahold of his wet, slobbery dick, placing it at the entrance of my tight asshole and then carefully lowering myself onto his giant rod.

"Oh fuck, oh fuck, oh fuck," I begin to murmer, struggling to allow my body acceptance of his enormous size. For now, the corn is simply teasing my rim, pressing playfully against the edge of my sphincter until finally it opens up in one quick movement and I drop down onto him.

"Cornholed at last!" Liplon shouts gleefully as his dick impales me.

I lean forward and grip tight onto the food's shoulders, my body still desperately trying to adjust to his girth. Every ounce of my being feels stretched tight, ready to snap at any moment under the pressure of his substantial thickness.

Instead, however, the pain and discomfort that surges through me begins to subside, replaced with a strange, aching pleasure that builds and builds with every slow grind of my hips. Eventually, my movements start to speed up, turning into full on swoops of passion against the muscular corn. By now the tightness of my ass has given way completely in a wave of utter bliss, the mystical power of an impending prostate orgasm blossoming within me to replace it.

The sensation starts low and deeps, somewhere within my belly before expanding out in a series of beautiful surges. With each pump of my body across his giant rod the feeling grows, moving down my arms and legs as I tremble excitedly.

I reach down and grab ahold of my dick, pumping my hand across my length in time with my movements of the corn's meaty cock up my rump.

"I'm so close," I yell. "Oh god, I'm gonna fucking blow my load!"

Suddenly, Liplon lifts me up off of him with his muscular arms, cutting short the waves of orgasm that had been building up within.

"What was that?" I groan. "I was gonna come."

"Not yet you aren't," laughs Liplon. "The key to every business transaction is making sure that both sides are happy, we're cumming together."

"Alright," I say with a playful grin, "you're on."

Suddenly, Liplon is flipping me over on the grass so that I'm now on my hands and knees, facing out towards the seemingly endless lights of the city below. The sight may be breathtaking, but it's not until the giant corn pushes his cock deep into my asshole from behind that I literally gasp out loud.

"Fucking hell!" I cry, my fingers gripping the grass before me as Liplon gets to work from behind.

The next thing I know, the handsome corn is pounding my butthole with everything that he's got, railing me with a ferocity unlike anything that I have ever seen. It feels incredible to be dominated by him, to know that he is much stronger and more powerful than me as he uses my ass for his burning vegetable pleasure.

It's not long before the familiar orgasmic sensations begin to bubble up within me once again, spilling out through my veins like simmering erotic venom. I'm quaking hard, every muscle in my body pulled tight and then breaking like waves.

"Harder!" I scream. "Pound my ass harder, corn!"

The vegetable does as he's told, never letting up for a second as he reams my depths with a sexual prowess that makes my toes curl.

I'm just about ready to cum when the food behind me slams forward with a powerful, final thrust, crying out with a howl that echoes around us for miles. The sound is immediately joined by a spastic crackle, a series of loud pops that rattle off in rapid succession.

I look back over my shoulder in shock to discover that Liplon is erupting in a fit of passion, the kernels across his body exploding into puffs of popcorn and then shooting off in every direction.

"I'm cumming!" I corn shouts.

Within me, I can feel the strangely pleasant snap of his cock popping as well, his orgasm displaying itself in a carnal preparation of snack food. He's filling me up with his seed, pumping load after load within me until finally there's just not enough room in my ass and the popcorn comes spilling out over the edges of my sphincter, scattering across the ground below like an overfilled popcorn machine at the local movie theatre.

"There's so much corn in my asshole!" I shriek, beating myself off with an untamed fury.

Suddenly, I'm cumming as well, my eyes rolling back into my head as a massive load of jizz erupts from the end of my swollen shaft. It splatters across the ground below me, mixing with the popcorn to form a warm pearly seasoning of gayness.

When I glance back over my shoulder once more I find myself alone on the cliff side, heaps of popcorn strewn everywhere but my handsome companion nowhere to be found. A strong wind blows and scatters the food, some of it whipping off into the air and swirling away into the distance.

In this moment, I realize that Liplon is truly gone.

I look up at the crowd before me, watching as the tears stream down their faces. I realize now that I too am crying, reminiscing of my night long ago with this agricultural lover.

"That's how I met Liplon," I say, reading the final words of his eulogy aloud, "when I met him at that conference I had no idea that this breathtaking living corn would change my heart, and my butthole, forever. He will be greatly missed."

I finish and then step back from the podium as a bugle begins to play, its bittersweet song soaring out across the grass of the cemetery. To my left, the coffin full of popcorn begins to lower slowly into the ground.

"I love you," I say under my breath, unable to take my eyes off of the oblong box until it is completely below the dirt. "I'll see you on the other side, and I'm ready for some corn hole."

FIRST BUCKAROO BILL POUNDED BY THE HANDSOME LIVING WHITE HOUSE

"Whoa," I announce loudly, frozen in the doorway of the Lincoln Bedroom, "It's good to be back."

My top secret service agent, Curpin, stands behind me, a man who has been hanging around for the last twenty years and never done me wrong. A man that I can trust with my life, but also keeps me in check when I need it. "Yes, sir, it is," he says.

It's not like I haven't been spending enough time in the White House over the last decade. When your wife is the Secretary of State and you're a former two term American president, it's not that difficult to find a reason for stopping in. The Lincoln Bedroom, however, hasn't belonged to me for quite a while.

"Would you like them to start moving in your things now, Bill?" asks Curpin, breaking my focus.

I glance back at my loyal agent. "Let's give it a moment, I want my wife to see this before we make it out own. There's something kind of nice about seeing this room as it was hundreds of years back."

A concerned look crosses Curpin's face. "I'm afraid that might be a while, sir. She's down in the Situation Room and we suspect she might be there until tomorrow."

"Tomorrow?" I question. "Must be serious."

Curpin nods.

"You think I should go down there and help out?" I continue.

Curpin's expression has a thinly veiled discomfort as he shakes his head. "May I speak freely, sir?"

I nod. "Of course, Curpin."

The secret service agent hesitates for a moment and then finally speaks. "You're not the president anymore, your wife is. Things like spending all night down in the Situation Room are not really part of your job."

I can't help the disappointed look that crosses my face, but it's impossible to stop because deep down I know that he's absolutely right. Summoning all of the calm I can muster, I straighten myself up and clear my head.

"Alright, so what's my new job?" I ask.

Curpin thinks about this for a moment and then shrugs. "Well, there have been plenty of First Ladies, but you're the First Buckaroo. You can make the job whatever you want it to be."

I take a deep breath, suddenly feeling the weight of this completely uncharted political position. The options are endless, but in a strange way, that's what makes figuring it out so difficult. I've spent plenty of time championing my own causes as a citizen, but by now all of the non-profits bearing my name are off and running on their own. My wife seems to have a handle on the task at hand downstairs, and that leaves me pretty much out of things to do.

"Maybe it's a blessing in disguise," Curpin offers. "I mean, you've worked so hard to get to where you are, Bill. Why not spend your time as the First Buckaroo just relaxing and having a little fun?"

I let out a long sigh, realizing that I might not have a choice in the matter.

"You want to play video games or something?" I ask.

My secret service agent doesn't know what to say at first, clearly not expecting the invitation.

"I'm sorry, sir," he counters, "I've been instructed to patrol the hallway outside after you're all settled in here."

"So it's just gonna be me on my own for the night?" I clarify.

Curpin nods.

"That's okay, that's okay," I offer solemnly, trying to brush away the feelings of depression as the begin to sink in. "You can go now, Curpin."

"You'll find something to fill your time," says the secret service agent warmly, then turns around and leaves me completely alone to stand in the doorway of this historic bedroom.

That night I barely sleep at all, tossing and turning in bed as I wrestle with the ever-darkening thoughts that fill my head.

I see the next four years of my life stretching out before me, boring and barren, a complete and utter departure from the time that I spent here in the White House as President not long ago. Political turmoil comes and goes, and I'm not a part of it, instead sitting alone and watching as the excitement passes me by.

I feel like a ghost here.

In the last few minutes before I fall asleep, I make a deal with myself. I'm not going to let the position of First Buckaroo mean nothing; for me, *and* for future men who find themselves with these big shoes to fill. I'm going to enjoy myself here in the White House if it's the last thing I do.

"What the hell is going on here?" Curpin asks, completely dumbfounded as he barrels out onto the White House lawn.

I glance over and smile, releasing the saxophone from my lips. "Just jamming a little bit," I tell him.

"Out here?" Curpin questions, nodding towards the White House fence that is currently surrounded by excited onlookers who wave and shout with patriotic enthusiasm.

"Gotta have a crowd!" I tell him. "They're lovin' these saxophone blues jams!"

"What about *these* guys?" Curpin shouts, pointing down at the muscular, thonged men who continue to grace the slip and slide that stretches out on the grass before me.

"They were here when I showed up!" I insist, but we both know this is far from the truth. "Hey listen, I'd really love to chat but the crowd is dying for more!"

I reach over and press play on the boom box next to me, the sound of heavy rock and roll immediately blasting out from the speakers once more at full volume. I hoist my saxophone and begin ripping out a wild solo once again, the citizens who've pressed themselves up against the White House fence immediately bursting into a raucous cheer. The handsome men who have been sliding up and down the White House lawn on my slip and slide kick things into high gear, as well, performing increasingly difficult rotations in their slides as the audience looks on in amazement.

"I'm sorry, sir. I know I told you to have a little fun, but this is not the type of behavior that the First Buckaroo should be participating in!" Curpin yells to me over the music.

I pretend not to hear him, losing myself in the sweet tunes as the thundering sound rolls over me.

"Sir!" yells Curpin, even louder now as he tries to get my attention.

I continue to ignore him, my saxophone wails hitting a fever pitch as the highest note possible soars out gracefully across the White House lawn.

Suddenly, everything stops. I pull the instrument away from my mouth and look down to find Curpin standing with the boom box in his hand, his finger planted firmly upon the pause button.

"Alright everybody, show's over!" he cries out, eliciting a moan of disappointment from the onlookers, as well as the slippery, shirtless hunks on the ground. "Orders from the President herself!"

I let out a long groan of my own now, recognizing that my wife will always have the last word in situations like this.

As the guys pack up their slip and slide I carefully put away my saxophone and then stoically follow Curpin back inside, my head lowered in defeat.

"Guess the White House isn't as fun as it used to be," I say.

We enter and I tell Curpin that I'm just going to head back to the bedroom and put away my instrument. He lets me go alone, and I relish this moment of freedom.

"I heard that," a voice suddenly comes floating out through the hallway around me.

I stop and turn around, looking for any sign of who could have possibly said this. As suspected, I'm all-alone, the high ceiling of this hallowed hall giving me a sense of smallness that pounds the point home even more.

"Hello?" I call out. "Who's there?"

A deep soulful laugh carries out down the hallway, drifting over my head as I spin in a circle. "Has it really been that long?" the voice asks. "I thought we were friends, Bill!"

Something about the way he says this actually strikes a chord somewhere deep down within my memory, a long forgotten friendship suddenly bubbling up to the forefront of my consciousness once again. A smile slowly begins to cross my face.

"Gorgon," I announce confidently. "How could I forget!"

"Good to have you back, Billy Boy," Gorgon announces.

Gorgon is an incredible living building, a man who I had my share of excitement with long, long ago. He's seen many Presidents come and go, seen wars and long times of peace. Of course, everyone else knows Gorgon by his more traditional name: The White House.

"I saw you get shut down out there on the lawn," the White House tells me. "If you'd been inside I could have said something, but I've got no control out on the lawn."

"It's alright," I assure him. "You've gotta stay neutral on those kind of things anyway."

The White House laughs, the hallway shaking slightly around me. "I mean, I *should* stay neutral, but you know how things can get some nights. This place is so stuffy, I miss having you around to party with."

"Well, I'm back," I tell Gorgon, "but I don't think I'm going to be partying very much these days. Between Curpin and President, I'm on a pretty tight leash."

"Good thing I've got plenty of room for privacy," says the living historical building.

As I recall, it's not unusual for the White House to be a bit mischievous, but there is something distinctly playful about his voice as he says this; flirty even.

I'd be lying if I said there wasn't a tension between us, but that's only natural when you spend as many long nights together in the Oval Office as we have. Nothing ever happened, of course, but it always felt like the sexual pressure could burst at any moment.

I suppose that's why it had been so easy to forget about Gorgon, in a strange way. I knew that if I dwelled on the erotic feelings we once shared they would do nothing but grow, so I must have just blocked the whole thing out entirely.

"You know, Madam President is down in the Situation Room again," offers the White House. "She's gonna be down there all night, just in case you wanted to go hang out in the Oval Office for a while and blow off some steam."

"I'm not sure about that…" I stammer, my party boy facade unexpectedly faltering. "You sure she won't come back?"

"I'm the White House," the living structure reminds me. "I think I'd know."

I let out a long sigh, finally giving in to the simmering arousal that continues to grow deep within me. "Alright, alright."

Instead of heading back to the Lincoln Bedroom I take a sharp left and stride confidently towards the Oval Office. I'm such a familiar face around here that nobody walking past me even gives a second glance, and despite my hard partying reputation, being the First Buckaroo gives you all the access you'd ever need.

There are two secret servicemen waiting outside the Oval Office door, but I simply nod and they let me inside where I am met with a powerful relic of my past. The room has an electricity to it, that's for sure, and while I'd grown used to spending my time in here as President, the familiarity has worn off enough that a surge of goose bumps make their way across my arms.

"How does it feel?" questions Gorgon.

"Like the good old days," I admit, strolling over to the presidential desk and running my fingers along the corner, taking it all in. "What about you? How does it feel to have me back inside of you?"

The White House hesitates for a moment, then finally answers with a simple. "Good. Really good."

In a moment of inspiration, I lift my saxophone to my lips and start to play a slow, romantic jam. The notes carry out from my instrument in a beautiful wave, filling the room with a lustful, aching sense of longing.

"You're so talented," Gorgon eventually tells me, interrupting my song.

It's now our never, I realize, my whole body trembling with anticipation. I'm face to face with a choice that could determine the next four years of my life here at the White House, maybe even the next eight. If I decide to make a move with Gorgon, then I know this life of governmental partying is where I need to be, but if I turn around now I might as well just settle down for good; no more sax in the front lawn, no more hunks on the slip and slide, no more horsin' around.

Finally, I make my choice.

"You know, this saxophone isn't the only thing that I'm good at blowing on," I tell the living American monument.

"Oh yeah?" the White House questions, playing along.

"Yeah," I tell him, placing my instrument on the desk and then walking around it, heading over towards the windows where the curtains hang down modestly and rustle in the slight breeze.

I reach out and grab the fabric that drapes the windows, then pull it open suddenly to reveal a massive cock protruding from the wall. I gasp at the sight of it, fully knowing it was there but never having the courage to take it in with my own eyes.

"You like what you see?" Gorgon asks.

I nod, then drop down onto my hands and knees, crawling towards the enormous member and taking it into my hand. Slowly but surely, I begin to stroke the White House off, letting the living building enjoy the tightness of my grip. The building starts to moan softly around me, clearly enjoying himself as I stroke faster and faster.

Eventually, I am beating Gorgon off at a furious pace, overwhelmed with aching homosexual lust for this handsome and well crafted structure.

I just can't help myself, opening wide and taking his shaft between my hungry lips.

"Oh fuck," the White House groans loudly.

I bob my head up and down his length a few times, savoring the salty taste of this historical member and considering all of the presidents from years past who only had the courage to look and not touch. I continue like this for a while, taking him with quick bursts of oral enthusiasm until eventually I push down all the way and swallow his member entirely. Gorgon's dick disappears completely within my neck in an expertly performed deep throat, consumed so fully that even *I* am amazed at my sexual dexterity. Somehow I've managed to relax enough that he slips easily past my gag reflex, plunging all the way inside as my face presses up against Gorgon's hard White House abs.

I hold the living building here for as long as I can and then finally pull back and release him with a loud, frantic gasp. I try desperately to collect myself, to reckon with the powerful homosexual lust that courses through my body, but it's just no use. No matter how hard I try to stop it, I can feel the frantic craving for White House cock consume me, turning me into a belligerent political dick addict who is willing to get off in any depraved way possible.

"I want you to fuck me," I tell Gorgon. "I want you to pound me up the ass the like bad little First Buckaroo that I am."

"With pleasure," the White House responds.

Immediately, I start to tear off my suit and tie, throwing my clothes to the side until I'm completely naked on my hands and knees. I turn around so that I'm facing away from the wall, as well as the massive cock that protrudes from its painted white surface.

"Do you want this former presidential ass?" I coo, wiggling my muscular butt playfully in front of the sentient building.

"Fuck yeah," the White House tells me.

I slowly back up against the wall, letting his massive cock slide up against my ass crack but not yet allowing him inside. I tease the White House with my buns, playfully moving back and forth while he aches for entry.

"Beg for it," I tell the White House.

"I want to fuck you so badly," Gorgon moans.

Heeding his words, I pull back and readjust so that the head of his swollen shaft is pressed up ever so slightly against the rim of my butthole. I hesitate for a moment, savoring this despite my cock crazed mental state, then finally just can't take it anymore as I slam myself down onto his rod.

I can't help but be shocked by the size of his gigantic member, letting out a startled yelp as Gorgon's massive cock impales me. I can feel his girth stretching my insides to the limit, my rectum struggling to contain all of this living object dick. I'd be lying if I said there was no twinge of discomfort as I allow him to take my asshole, but the longer I allow the White House to pummel my depths, the more this sensation transforms into a throbbing, pleasurable ache.

Soon enough, I an slamming back against him with all of my might, allowing him access to parts of my body that have never been explored until this very moment. I can feel a strange warmth starting to pulse through me in a series of waves, starting small at first and then growing bigger and bigger with every successive slam up my asshole. It's not long before I realize that this strange new sensation is one of prostate orgasm, the tension that has built within my body suddenly on the verge of boiling over.

I reach down and begin to pump my fist across the length of my own cock, matching my movements to the thrusts within my ass. I'm trembling now, my body reeling with all of these foreign sensations as they beg for release.

"Oh my god, I'm so close," I inform the living piece of American history. "I'm gonna cum so fucking hard!"

"Wait!" the White House tells me, causing me to halt mid thrust. "Don't cum yet."

"But why?" I ask him, aching to explode.

"I want you to cum inside of me," the enormous living building tells me. "I want you to cum up my ass."

"Okay," I concede, then glance back over my shoulder at him playfully. "You first."

Immediately, I start to jackhammer back against the firm White House cock as hard as I can, using every ounce of my strength to send his rod straight up my sphincter. It's not long before the entire building is quaking with orgasmic pressure, just waiting to be released.

"Do it!" I scream. "Cum up my fucking butthole like the filthy gay former President that I am!"

Suddenly, the White House is exploding within me, his massive load blasting up into my butthole in a series of spastic pumps. When there's no space left to contain it, I can feel his warm spunk squirt out from the edges of my tightly packed ass, running down my crack and dripping onto the sacred floor of the Oval Office below.

Finally, I move away from the wall and Gorgon's dick slides out of me in a cascade of pearly white semen.

"Find my ass," groans the White House, "it's in the rose garden, behind a bush. Right next to the Situation Room escape hatch."

I know exactly where he's talking about, and although I'd climbed up through the hidden escape tunnel several times during our seasonal drills, I'd never once noticed a butthole.

As quickly as I can, I throw on my clothes and scramble out the door, not wanting to wait even the slightest bit longer before I blow my load.

I almost forget my saxophone, but hesitate just before heading out in the hall just long enough to grab it. The next thing I know, I am making my way down the seemingly endless twisting corridors of my lover, trying to avoid eye contact with anyone who might possibly ask what I'm up to.

Unfortunately, I'm spotted quickly.

"Bill!" calls out Curpin, running up from behind me. "Where were you? I've been looking all over for you!"

I turn around to face him and quickly adjust my hair, attempting to look as together as possible despite the disheveled nature of my attire. "I got lost," I lie.

Curpin just stares at me blankly. "Sir, you spent eight years here as president and you *still* don't know your way around?"

I've been caught red handed and I know it, and if I don't think fast then Curpin is certain to report this to my wife. If that happens, I'll be grounded to the Lincoln Bedroom until the next election season.

Suddenly, a wave of calm washes over me as I realize that there is only one way out of this. I need to tell the truth.

"Alright," I finally say, "I wasn't taking my saxophone back. I was in the Oval Office."

A look of solemn confusion crosses Curpin's face. "What were you doing in the Oval Office?" he questions.

I take a deep breath. "I was letting the White House fuck me up the ass," I explain.

"Gorgon?" Curpin exclaims, shocked.

I nod. "Listen, Curpin, I know this seems crazy and everything but I need you to hear me out. What me and Gorgon have is something special, it's not just a flash in the pan."

Curpin is listening intently, watching as my eyes fill with tears.

"I love him," I admit.

"And what about your wife?" questions my trusted secret service agent.

"I love her, too," I exclaim. "I think that the three of us could make something work, I really do."

Curpin considers this for a moment, thinking long and hard about all the information I've presented to him. Still, he says nothing.

"I need to go out to the rose garden and cum in the White House's butthole," I continue. "I need to finish what I started."

Now Curpin is crying, too, my long time friend now realizing that he is in the presence of true passion unfolding.

Curpin nods. "Go, just go," he says with a teary smile.

"Thank you," I offer, turning to leave and then stopping abruptly. "You're the best secret service agent I've ever had," I tell him.

"You're the best First Buckaroo," he jokes with a playful smile. "Now go show that butthole you've still got it!"

The next thing I know I am sprinting full speed through the White

House, twisting and turning down the long corridors until finally I arrive at the door to the rose garden. I push through it, enjoying the warm sun and fresh air against my skin.

"Over there," the White House suddenly pipes up, "behind that bush."

I make my way over the edge of the building, sliding behind a large rose bush and then kneeling down to inspect the outside wall. I spot it almost immediately, a tiny puckered butthole staring back at me in all of its handsome glory. A startled gasp escapes my lips.

"What are you waiting for," Gorgon coos playfully.

I unbuckle my pants and slide them down, then push myself up against the hard wall, running my hands across the solid craftsmanship of this elegant older building. The rim of Gorgon's butthole welcomes my cock as I tease against the edge of his tightness, then moments later I push forward into the warm political anus.

Immediately, I get to work pumping in and out of the White House's taut ass, slamming into his rectum with animalistic fury until, finally, I just can't hold back any longer. I throw my head towards the sky and let out a howl of ecstasy, jizz erupting from my shaft and filling my gorgeous gay lover to the brim.

"Oh my fucking god," I cry, the sensations within my body to just overwhelming not to vocalize.

When I finally finish I fall over to the side, but where I expected the ground to catch me there is suddenly none. Frantically, I try to catch my balance but before I can I'm tumbling down into a long metal shaft that I immediately recognize as the presidential escape route from the Situation Room. Even over end I flip, rolling over myself in the air several times before hitting a metal vent and bursting through. There is a loud thud as I slam into the middle of a conference table, and an entire room of high-ranking political figures lets out yelps of shock, my wife included.

Struggling to collect myself, I look around in a daze to find that I've landed in the Situation Room, right in the middle of the conference table. On a screen before me is the large face of a notorious Russian diplomat.

"Bill... is that you?" the diplomat questions.

I nod, clearing my throat and trying to pull my pants back on. My saxophone was crushed under my weight during the fall. "Yeah, it's me."

The diplomat smiles. "You know... I've always said that you can trust someone who knows how to party. Forget what I said earlier, we will agree to stand down."

The American politicians around me exchange glances of excitement.

"Really?" I question.

"Of course," says the diplomat with a nod.

The screen shuts off as the video call is disconnected, causing the entire room to burst out in uproarious applause.

I guess there's a time and place for me to horse around in the White House after all.

POUNDED BY PRESIDENT BIGFOOT

It's weird to look back and remember a time when bigfeet were still considered a thing of mystery; a myth, a legend. Many years ago, almost too many to remember at this point, the entire species were considered to be nothing more than a figment of imagination born from the minds of frightened campers in the deep dark woods.

I was just a teenager when it finally happened. The bigfeet, or sasquatch as they are sometimes called, held a massive press conference and exposed themselves to the outside world, seeking a truce with humankind as their land became further and further encroached upon.

There was desperation in their attempt to integrate into our society, but for the most part they were welcomed with open arms. Soon enough, it wasn't uncommon to see bigfeet working in restaurants, pumping gas, or even holding small government positions.

That is, of course, until Gardook Yuldok hit the scene.

Yuldok was a beautiful brown bigfoot, large even for his species. The creature became notable after co-writing a few pop hits that cracked into the top forty. Eventually, he released a record of his own titled, "It's Lonely Out Here In The Forest" which became an immediate classic with even the most jaded of hipsters. Something about the bigfoot experience began to resonate with people across the globe, and soon enough Yuldok became a household name.

But nothing could have prepared mankind for what would come next.

Eventually, rumors started to buzz about Yuldok campaigning for office. Technically, as someone born within the United States, he was allowed to run for the position of president, although the idea still seemed far-fetched. After all, we had spent centuries with humans as the leader of the free world, not bigfeet.

But the rumors were true, and Yuldok won by a landslide after staying true to a platform of environmental activism and fiscal conservation. History was made, and I was lucky enough to see it happen.

Growing up, I knew always wanted to be involved in politics. Sparked by my fifth grade class election, when I won by a landslide against a guy with an absolutely terrifying set of braces, climbing the social ladder has fascinated me like nothing else. After my win I was hooked, finding motivation to excel with the idea that, someday, all of these accomplishments would be vetted as I was on my way to becoming the first openly gay president of the United States. Of course, things never turn out exactly the way that we think that they will.

Instead, I became a journalist, and damn good at it. When I started out I was mostly covering filler stories, but eventually I worked my way into the coveted position of chief political correspondent of a very successful news blog. I'm a guy who's willing to get down and dirty and get what he wants, even if that means bending a few rules to get there.

I got my job in my mid twenties; right around the time that President Yuldok began to enter his second term. Our blog was getting bigger, but I still remember the feeling of shock that radiated through my body when I first learned that we had landed an interview with the president himself.

When I realized that, due to my position, I would be the one at the helm of this historic opportunity, I almost had a heart attack. But, I somehow managed to hold it together enough to prepare some direct and hard-hitting questions for the first bigfoot president.

I'll be the first to admit it, most of my journalistic skills are based on the simple fact that, unlike most of my aging, wrinkled contemporaries, I'm a handsome young gay man. It certainly doesn't hurt to have my looks when trying to press a few buttons. This could come in especially handy in regards to President Yuldok, amidst rumors that the creature was gay due to his lack of a first lady.

The president tried to play it off coolly, suggesting that he was just to busy to find a suitable mate, but the general public wasn't buying it. The only thing that saved Yuldok was that he was already the first non-human President of the United States, making the idea that he could possibly be the first gay one less than newsworthy in the eyes of many.

When the day of the interview finally came, I was more than ready to meet the world's first bigfoot president, but nothing could have prepared me for what was about to happen, changing the way that I looked at love and lust forever.

"Identification please." The security guard asks me as I show him my shiny new White House press credentials.

"Right here." I tell him nervously. "First day."

"Only day." The guard says, cracking a smile. He runs my badge along a strange red scanner on the counter in front of him. It beeps twice, then he hands my card back to me.

"Just follow this hallway until you see the big white doors, there will be four secret service officers there to greet you. They'll take you inside the oval office when President Yuldok is ready." He says.

I start to walk away from the counter and then stop, unable to help myself as I turn back around and lean in towards the guard. I lower my voice amid the hustle and bustle of the first floor office lobby. "What's president Yuldok like?" I ask.

The guard thinks for a moment, apparently weighing a whole series of possible consequences in his head and then finally says. "Intense."

I nod, then continue onward into the hallowed halls of the infamous west wing. For a political junkie like myself, there could be nothing more incredible that being here in this notorious building and basking in the incredible sense of patriotic history. I gaze in wonder at the portraits that line the hallway as I pass by, various presidents long since dead who once walked these grounds, making decisions that would forever change the world.

I round a corner and immediately find myself face to face with the four secret service officers who were mentioned earlier. They check my credentials a second time and then instruct me to sit on a couch positioned just outside the door, which I do gladly, gripping my notebook and small audio recorder tightly in my hands.

From where I sit and can see movement under the door to the oval office, a shadow that paces back and forth within. There is a voice speaking loudly, deep in the midst of some heated phone call that I'm just barely out of earshot to hear.

The pacing stops.

My heart immediately begins to quicken within my chest, pounding harder and harder as I can hear large, lumbering footsteps approach the door before me. I try desperately to prepare myself for the presence of this glorious creature, but the second President Yuldok opens the door he completely takes my breath away.

The large, hairy beast smiles at me and then gives a nod, "Allen Bennet?"

I don't say anything, frozen in complete awe.

"Mr. Bennet?" The president repeats. "Your blog requested an interview?"

Suddenly, everything comes rushing back to me and I regain control of my senses. "Yes!" I gasp. "I'm sorry about that, yes, I'm Allen."

I stand up and shake President Yuldok's massive hairy hand, immediately taken by his powerful grip. As strange as it sounds, there is something incredibly sexy about the president's beastly presence, instantly creating an overwhelming sense of submission to his monstrous size. I'm trying to remain as professional as possible, but I find it difficult to quell the steady ache of my slightly hardening cock.

What are these feelings? I desperately ask myself.

Despite their integration into our society, relationships between bigfeet and humans are still very taboo, and a gay relationship of that sort is even more so. Not that any of this even matters, because at the end of the day, he is the bigfoot president and I am just a lowly blogger.

However, I can't help but notice the way that Yuldok's large bigfoot hand lingers on mine as he leads me into the office. Maybe the rumors about our president were true, after all.

"Come on in." President Yuldok says. "Have a seat."

The handsome bigfoot politician sits at a large oak desk on the far side of the office. There are two chairs placed across from the desk to face him but, other than that, the room is almost entirely void of furniture, just a large rug in the center and bookshelves lining the walls.

"You like what I've done with the place?" Yuldok asks. "There used to be some couches in here, I don't know if you've seen pictures or not. Anyway, I'm just too big and I like to pace around when I talk, so I moved the couches out. I kept on tripping over them; broke one, actually."

I sit down in the chair across from the hairy president. "Do you find it hard to adjust?" I ask, turning on my tape recorder with a firm click. "You're the first non-human president, there must be all sorts of things around here that need to be custom fitted for bigfeet. Larger pens maybe?"

Yuldok smiles. He's even more handsome up close, muscular with shiny fur and what seems to be a permanent devilish twinkle in his eye. The creature instantly commands the room, and he knows it.

"I'll tell you all about it." Says the president. "But first you'll have to turn off that recorder."

I look at him dumbfounded for a moment, not exactly sure where he's headed with this, but do as I'm told. "You don't allow recorders in here?" I ask, confused.

"Not for this interview." Yuldok tells me, leaning back in his large wooden chair.

We sit in silence for a moment while Yuldok takes me in with his deep, soulful eyes. I'm not sure what to do, wondering if he expects me to talk first and then finally offering, "This is a nice… desk you've got here."

Yuldok smiles. "Thank you. Now how about a compliment for you?" The large creature offers.

I'm utterly perplexed, but humor him. "Sure, why not." I say.

"You're an utterly gorgeous man." Yuldok tells me.

I immediately blush, my heart kicking into double time again as I realize that my suspicions are looking more and more to be correct about my hairy, gay president.

"Why are you telling me this?" I ask him, trying to keep my cool.

"I've seen you before, online." President Yuldok explains. "Your video blogs are very good, and you turn me on."

"Thank you." I say.

"Did you know that not only am I the first non-human president, but I'm also the first president to never have a first lady?" Yuldok asks.

I nod.

"Do you know why that is?" He continues.

I know the answer but I don't want to say it, terrified that I'm about to walk into some kind of verbal trap that has been meticulously laid out for me by this cunning sasquatch politician. I take a deep breath. "Because you're gay?" I finally ask.

Yuldok grins and looks back down at the recorder, double-checking that the red light is off. "Yes." He finally answers.

I'm speechless, reeling somewhere between disappointment that I'm clearly not allowed to report this, but elation that I might actually have a chance with this incredible, presidential beast. "I am too." I finally tell him.

Yuldok nods. "Yes, I know. With the secret service at my disposal, it's fairly easy to drum up information on just about anyone. After seeing you on your blog, I've decided that you would be the perfect candidate for my needs."

"Candidate?" I ask.

Yuldok rolls his eyes and chuckles. "I'm sorry, that sounds so sterile. I'll try to leave my politics outside of the room when we're in here together. Maybe 'lover' is a better word."

"I'm sorry," I admit. "I don't entirely follow."

"I'd like to fuck you." Yuldok says, calmly and completely straight faced.

Despite his alpha swagger, the president's bluntness has finally gone too far and I actually find myself a little bit offended by his offer. Everything about this is just too formal, too… strange.

I can tell that he sees this in my face, but his collected domineer doesn't falter for a second.

"Why would I let you do that?" I ask, flustered.

Yuldok doesn't miss a beat. "Because I'm hot, gay, intelligent and I'm the fucking president; because I'm a rare commodity and I know my value. Because I can."

My jaw nearly drops as he says this, partially offended by his confidence but also, despite my best efforts, a little impressed. Being as handsome as I am, I've never had a gay man come at me without just a hint of desperation lurking somewhere, but Yuldok clearly doesn't need me, he wants me.

I suddenly realize that I'm rock hard in my pants craving the touch of this powerful beast. He's so handsome and secure in that lush brown fur and those piercing dark eyes, I can't even imagine a world were I wouldn't be completely swept away the second that I saw him.

"I don't think so, let's keep this interview professional." I force myself to say, despite the fact that I want him inside of me more than anything right now.

There is a twinkle in Yuldok's eyes as I say this, then a long pause before he finally responds with a simple, "Fine." He taps a button on his desk and suddenly the doors behind me are swinging open, leading back out of the oval office.

I sit in my chair for a moment, stunned that he wasn't going to try harder to get into my pants before it suddenly dawns on me that he doesn't need to. President Yuldok is the leader in this exchange, not me, which is a rare situation for a me to find myself in.

"You can go." Yuldok adds, driving the point home. "The interview's over."

I sigh, but don't move an inch. "What do you want from me?" I finally ask.

"I told you. Sex." Yuldok answers calmly. "You said no, so now you're leaving."

"I'm sorry." I blurt, shocking even myself. "What are the details?"

President Yuldok winks at me with his large, sasquatch eye, a disturbingly cocky move that he can somehow get away with easily. "I get to fuck you." Says the hairy creature. "You get the honor of having been fucked by me."

Finally, I just can't take it anymore, his alpha arrogance pushing me over the edge from which there is no return. I want him to take me right here, right now.

"I'll do it." I blurt, my heart nearly pounding out of my chest. "I'll service you like the filthy gay human that I am."

"Are you sure that you're up for the job?" He asks.

"Yes." I tell him, the word falling from my lips in a soft moan.

Yuldok stands up from his desk and then walks slowly around to stand behind me, placing his strong, hairy hands on either shoulder in a subtle display of dominance.

I can hear Yuldok unzipping his fly, pulling it down slowly and then releasing his cock, which he lays across my shoulder in all of it's thick, brown glory. I turn my head to look at the stiffening rod and then gasp aloud, reeling in shock from its substantial girth.

"It's incredible." I mumble.

"You know what they say about big feet." The president tells me.

Slowly, I turn in my chair to face Yuldok, looking up with big gay doe eyes as I take his cock into my hands, noting the stark contrast of my skin tone and his brown fur. His dick is so huge that I can barely wrap my hand around it, but I do my best, gripping him tightly and slowly beginning to pump up and down over the length of his beastly shaft.

Yuldok is clearly enjoying himself, closing his eyes and leaning back as a low, sensual moan escapes his lips. He starts to move his hips along with me, synchronizing himself with the strokes of my hand while I cradle his balls with the other. Eventually, my pumping grows faster and faster until finally my hand is simply not enough and I take him hungrily into my mouth, swallowing as much of his massive dick as I can muster.

My lips are stretched to the brink as I attempt to take down his python, pushing myself onto it with everything that I've got until the member finally hits my gag reflex and I find myself retching loudly. I pull back and take a huge gasp of air, slightly embarrassed but feinding for more.

Yuldok actually chuckles to himself as I collect my wits, then places his large hands behind my head and helps to push me back down onto his rod again. I'm ready now, taking him deep and then relaxing as the head of his mammoth cock presses up against my gag reflex. This time I manage to slide past it, plunging his cock down much deeper than any dick I've ever taken, and eventually I find myself with Yuldok's hard bigfoot abs pressed up against my face, his cock disappearing completely within me. Tears well up in my eyes as he holds me there, a natural reaction to consuming such a massive wand of flesh, but somehow his rough treatment of my face dose nothing but turn me on even more.

I'm trembling with desire, my throat full of dick and my cock aching to blow its hot load. I want him to fuck me up my ass; I want to get off.

Yuldok pushes my head up and down a bit, controlling my movements as I pleasure his shaft and then finally, just as I'm about to run out of air, he lets me up to breathe.

"I love that fucking big bigfoot cock." I tell him desperately. "But I need it in my asshole, I need it so bad."

"Is that how you address your superior?" Yuldok asks sternly in his deep, booming voice.

"I need you in my asshole, Mr. Bigfoot President." I repeat, formally.

Immediately, he lifts me up from the chair and then bends me over his desk so that I'm now overlooking his incredible view of the White House lawn. Yuldok fiercely pulls down my jeans and boxer briefs, exposing my gay ass to the cool office air.

"Oh my god, I can't believe I'm doing this." I moan. "I'm such a bad, bad boy."

"Yes you are." Yuldok says, slapping my rump hard. He takes my hips in his strong hands and then skillfully aligns his thick rod with my puckered hole. Moments later he's pushing forward, stretching my tightness around his massive shaft while it slides deeper and deeper into my depths, finally coming to rest at the bottom and holding me here for a moment, savoring me. I let out a long moan, my hands gripping tightly onto the edge of the desk as Yuldok begins to pump in and out of me with his Bigfoot cock, moving slowly at first and then gaining speed with his expert railing.

I close my eyes tight, bracing myself against his movements as well as the waves of pleasure that quickly begin to pulse through my body.

"That feels so good Mr. President." I groan. "I love taking that big hairy dick."

I feel another hard slap against my ass and look back at him over my shoulder, reveling in the incredible sight of this amazing figure plowing me, using me however he sees fit. I'm here for his pleasure now, a servant to his deviant gay desires and yet somehow, I feel free. Free to express the deep dark secret that I've carried around with me for longer than I can remember, that I want nothing more than to be dominated by a strong, muscular sasquatch.

By now, Yuldok is hammering me with all of his strength, every pump against my backside causing the desk to rattle and shake. I'm shaking as well, my body struggling to cope with the torrent of overwhelming sensations that are blooming with unstoppable beauty from my prostate. An orgasm is not far behind, and I reach down between my legs, stroking my dick to help myself along but, before I can, Yuldok suddenly pulls out of me and flips me over.

Maneuvered by his large, muscular arms, I suddenly find myself on my back with my legs in the air, spread wide open while Yuldok slams into my butthole with an animalistic fury. With every thrust my legs bounce in the air, framing Yuldok's chiseled bigfoot face.

"You're doing great work here." Yuldok tells me with a cocky wink. "Best interview I've ever had."

"Thank you, sir." I tell him.

"I've got an advanced task for you, though." He says. "I hope you're up for it."

"I'm up for it." I moan, the powerful feelings suddenly getting the best of me as I begin to tremble again, wild spasms shooting up and down my body. "I'm up for anything. My body is yours."

Yuldok pulls out. "That's what I thought." He takes his gigantic rod in his hands and then lowers it slightly, pushing forward until the head of his shaft presses lightly against the puckered entrance of my already reamed back door. Next to his cock, however, I can feel something else; something quietly pulled from some inside the bigfoot president's oak desk.

"Wait, are you?" I stammer, trying desperately to collect my thoughts. "Is this?"

"Double penetration?" Yuldok answers with a smirk. "Yes. You're going to take my giant bigfoot dick *and* the official presidential butt plug at the same time."

"I've never done it before." I admit. "A DP."

"It's about time you learned." Yuldok tells me, pushing forward against the rim of my tightness. My body resists him at first, and then moments later my asshole expands around his shaft and the plastic plug, spreading wide while I groan in a mixture of extreme pleasure and dull pain. I try my best to relax as he enters me, but his cock is so huge that it's impossible not to respond to its size. The deeper he slides with the dildo, however, the better it starts to feel, and by the time he comes to rest down within the depths of my anus the sensation has become a wonderful, overpowering fullness that envelopes me entirely.

"Fuck." I whimper. "I can't believe I've got a dick and a dildo up my ass at the same time."

"Believe it." Yuldok says, pulling out and then thrusting forward again, this time a little rougher and more deliberate. He does it again and again, plowing me harder every time as I squeal with delight until eventually he finds a nice, steady rhythm within me. I like watching him as he works, letting my eyes bask in the glory of his impeccable, refined abs and muscular hairy shoulders. I reach down and run my hands along the dark fur of Yuldok's rippling chest, unable to stop myself as a flustered gasp escapes my lips.

The two of us are now moving together in perfect synchronicity, our bodies tethered by lustful movements. There is a pleasant tension building up inside of me again, an orgasmic wave of prostate pleasure just waiting to break, but I want to cum while riding on top of him.

"Lie down." I tell Yuldok breathlessly, momentarily pulling his massive cock out of my asshole, the dildo popping out with it.

He does what he's told without hesitation, turning around and lying flat across his presidential desk while I climb up onto him, my feet planted firmly on either side. Without hesitation, I squat down and impale my gay asshole with his huge dick.

"Oh god damn, that feel's so fucking good." Yuldok tells me in his deep voice.

I start to swoop down against him hard, focusing intently on the strange sensation within my ass while I rapidly beat my cock.

It's not long before my body is trembling hard, quakes of lust shooting up and down my limbs while I enter the final stages of launch.

"You're gonna make me cum!" I scream. "Fuck!"

Suddenly, a wave of unbridled pleasure hits me like a train, causing me to throw my head back and let out a frantic howl of ecstasy. I'm quaking on top of the bigfoot president, my entire body enveloped by a series of powerful, spastic convulsions. Hot ropes of jizz shoot from the head of my cock, splattering everywhere. My eyes roll back into my head and I clench my teeth, the sensation almost too much to handle as I ride it out and then finally relaxing as it subsides into a pleasant, satisfied warmth.

Yuldok is right behind me, railing away at my tight asshole then suddenly pushing up into me and holding, every muscle in his body clenched in unison as a massive ejection of cum blasts from his cock. It fills me with a strange warm and quickly becomes too much to contain, squirting out from the tightly packed rim of my asshole in white, milky streaks. His dick twitches with every pump, ejecting a series of large payloads before finally settling down.

Once Yuldok is entirely finished, I climb up off of him, letting his jizz splatter out onto the desk below me. He stands with me and takes me into his muscular, hairy arms, kissing me deeply.

"You did a great job today." He whispers in my ear. "We can do the real interview as soon as tomorrow."

I smile, then respond with a simple, "Thank you, Mr. President."

I pull my clothes back on and then, after another quick kiss from Yuldok, turn around and make my way out of the oval office.

POUNDED IN THE BUTT BY MY LEAKED MASHLY ADDISON DATA

The wave of fear that washes over me when I hear news of the hack is something that I will never forget, a sickening dread that soaks into every ounce of my soul.

I'm lounging on a massive couch in my Washington D. C home, taking a well-needed break after a long day in the senate, while my wife, Tilpa, prepares dinner in the kitchen behind me.

On the television is my typical nightly news digest, a barrage of stories that I should probably be paying more attention to but simply can't find the motivation right now. I don't know how anyone could after the stress that I go though every day as a high level government official.

"How do you want your steak cooked, honey?" my wife calls out from the kitchen, apparently ready to throw our meat on the grill.

"Medium rare," I call back, not even taking a moment to avert my eyes from the screen before me.

It's not because I'm trying to be rude or callous, it's because I can't even bare to look at her right now with the knowledge of what I've done, the way that I've betrayed this woman who has never done anything but care for me from the bottom of her heart.

My wife and me have been dead in the bedroom for a while now, and I'll be the first to admit that it's my own fault. With all of this stress from work, I've become an irritable man and snapped at her more than enough times to make the sparks of attraction fade away into nothing. I'm not surprised that seldom wants to sleep with me, because I no longer want to sleep with her.

At least she tries, but these days it just seems to make things worse. Long story short, I've lost interest.

Still, my sex drive is something that needs to be satiated, and thanks to a website by the name of Mashly Addison, I can get that fix whenever I need it.

Mashly Addison is a website for husbands and wives who are looking to cheat on their partner with a bigfoot lover, a term that has recently been coined as "getting mashed." The site itself is fairly simple to use, even for an old, out-of-touch politician like myself. I just gave them my credit card information, social security number, and cock size, and then the next thing I knew I had a beautiful new profile that was ready for action.

It wasn't long before I started to get my first messages, but I can't deny that most of the time I was the one who would start the conversation. I absolutely love my wife, but at this point she simply can't satisfy me the way that a hunky, gay bigfoot can, and they are swarming Mashly Addison.

Even when Tilpa and me *do* find a rare moment of romance between the sheets, I can't help but let my thoughts drift away to some wild bigfoot fantasy, imagining what it would feel like if my ass was getting reamed from behind by a massive, armed-sized bigfoot cock.

It's usually then that I cum, but somehow I feel as though my wife can sense the betrayal of what's going on in my head. There is never a catharsis between us, never a moment of relief that allows us to overcome this hump of marital displeasure.

And so I continue to cheat, continue to sneak around behind the back of my loving wife as I meet up with a never-ending string of horny bigfeet on Mashly Addison. Eventually, my ass feels though its going to fall right out of me, pounded into submission by the constant parade of hairy bigfoot wang, but still I keep going, trying to fill a void somewhere deep within my cold conservative heart.

All the while, I never even think about my wife, about how hurt she would be if she discovered that I would rather run to the arms of another instead of try to work out the issues between us.

Thirty years of marriage, and this is the respect that I show her.

Back on the living room couch, I get the distinct feeling that I should be more upset than I am with myself, that I should be even more sad and distraught about the way I've treated my beautiful partner, Tilpa. If this were a movie then a single, salty tear would slowly appear in the corner of my eye, hovering for a moment before it cascades poetically down the side of my face in a salty streak.

But this is not a movie, and instead of a tear across my face there grows a subtle smile. I can't help it, the grin growing wider and wider as I realize that, for all of the terrible things I've done, both personally and professionally as a ruthless politician, I've gotten away with all of it.

"Breaking news tonight as a massive hacking scandal rocks the internet," a voice suddenly sounds from the television before me. I young woman sits behind a news desk and looks directly at the camera as it zooms in towards her. "I'm Mimmy Beefs. Dating site Mashly Addison has been hacked by an activist group, who have released the personal information of all members across the internet tonight, including many prominent government officials."

I literally spit my drink out as I hear this, the soda erupting from my mouth in a misty plume that fills the air before me.

"Is everything okay, Kurps?" my wife asks walking over from the kitchen to check on me.

I scramble to regain my composure. "Yeah, yeah, everything is fine. I was just watching the news and I choked a bit."

"Are you sure you're okay?" Tilpa continues, genuinely concerned as she walks over.

Frantically trying to get her to leave the room and not notice the television, I completely lose my cool. "Get the hell out of here, I'm fine! I told you, I'm fine!"

Tilpa stops, staring at me awkwardly as she attempts to decipher my strange behavior.

"Not your typical dating website, Mashly Addison specialized in providing a service to sad, unattractive men who think that their misery has more to do with their partner than their own self hatred. Cheating spouses use the website for discreet hookups with all kinds of creatures; bigfeet, dinosaurs, and unicorns, most of whom are also cheaters themselves," the news anchor continues.

Suddenly, my wife looks up at the screen, something clicking deep within her brain.

"I said, I'm fine," I announce, but Tilpa's attention it locked solidly on the television now, and there is nothing I can do about it.

"If you would like to see if your partner has been using this website, there are many search engines available," explains the anchor. "The data of anyone who used the website is now free to be discovered by anyone curious enough to look."

I notice my wife glance over at me from the side of her eyes, clearly more than a little suspicious.

"What?" I shout. "You think I am on Mashly Addison now?"

"You're telling me that you're not?" Tilpa asks.

I shake my head, "I'd never betray your trust like that."

"Oh really?" Tilpa continues.

My heart is hammering hard in my chest now, a thunderous rhythm that grows faster and faster with every passing minute.

"I swear on my life," I tell her, lying through my teeth.

Tilpa thinks about this for a moment, considering whether or not she actually believes me. "Then I guess you have no reason to mind if I search for you name then?" my wife counters.

I feel as though I'm about to pass out, my entire body buzzing with a nervous anxiety. I'm completely trapped, unable to stop this cascade of lies from inevitably being revealed to the world at large.

"I don't… Maybe, we should…" I stammer, unable to find my words.

"That's what I thought," Tilpa suddenly says. She stands up and walks back into the kitchen, where her laptop sits open on the counter and displays the recipe for tonight's dinner.

I immediately spring to my feet and follow close behind, desperately trying to convince her to drop this whole thing and get back to grilling up my delicious and juicy steak. "I can't believe you think I would be on that horrible website!" I protest. "This is so offensive!"

"Yeah, yeah, yeah," my wife mocks. She takes her laptop and opens up a new window, typing in a quick search for "Mashly Addison database." She has no problem finding what she's looking for.

"So if I type in your name, nothing's going to turn up?" Tilpa asks angrily.

I remain silent.

"Answer me!" my wife screams.

"Go ahead," I finally tell her. "Search for me."

Without hesitation, Tilpa types in my name, Kurps Krimple.

I watch in absolute horror as the website begins to load, the computer sorting through millions and millions of files for this tiny chain of letters that could utterly destroy my life. Not only is my marriage on the line, but my political carrier as well. As a conservative, family-values republican, the revelation that I routinely enjoy anal reaming from a homosexual bigfeet is not something that I could ever live down.

There is a loud mechanical ding as the search finishes, displaying its results.

I am in utter shock. "Name not found," I read aloud, trying my best to hide my overwhelming surprise.

Tilpa appears to be just as shocked as I am.

"I told you," I finally scoff.

My wife lets out a long sigh. "I'm sorry, Kurps. I don't know what got into me."

We just look at each other for a moment, a strange tension flowing between us until finally Tilpa returns to the kitchen and continues preparing dinner.

Later that night, I find myself still lounging on the living room couch long after my wife has excused herself to bed. This is usually how it goes, and unspoken rule that neither of us has to lay down next to each other while the other one is awake. Sometimes, I'll even pretend to fall asleep out here like it was an accident, even though both of us are plainly aware that I did it on purpose.

Tonight, however, I really do find myself glued to the television. The reports on the leak from Mashly Addison keep pouring in, various news commentators taking their turn at picking apart what this could mean for the thousands of cheating men and women who've been caught with their pants down. It appears that there's not much to know about the situation yet, but they still manage to find a way to stretch things out for the sake of ratings, of course.

Most frustrating, however, is the fact that despite all of this information, not a single person has been able to address my one burning question in any way. Why wasn't my data leaked to the public?

There is no doubt in my mind that my information should have been part of that database. I had used the Mashly Addison service several times and my credit card had been charged for it, leaving the type of paper trail in my wake that is not easy to ignore. It's as if my data just picked up and walked off on its own.

Suddenly, my cell phone rings.

I glance over at the wall clock, noticing that it's already close to midnight, a little late to be getting a call from an unknown number.

"Hello?" I say, picking up to phone as a strange anxiety floods my body.

"Kurps, it's great to hear your voice," comes a rich, soulful tone.

"Who is this?" I ask, slightly annoyed.

"I bet your wondering why your data wasn't found in the Mashly Addison dump, aren't you?" the voice asks.

"How did you know that?" I question.

"If you want the anwser, you'll have to come and meet me tonight," says the voice.

"Tonight?" I ask. "It's late, I'm already in bed."

"Well, it's still before midnight so, knowing you, you're actually out on the couch trying to avoid your wife," says the voice.

I stand up abruptly, walking over to the window next to me and looking out into the darkened yard of my mansion. It's hard to see anything out there, but as far as I can tell there is no way for someone to be peeping into this room right now.

"Who are you?" I ask again.

"Meet me and you'll find out," the voice reaffirms. "If not, your information might just show up somewhere that you don't want it."

"Oh god," I groan.

"Is that a yes?" the voice asks.

I hesitate for a moment. "Yeah, it is," I finally tell him.

"Good," the voice replies. "I'm in the warehouse district, come alone. 1342 15th street."

There is a click and then a soft hum as the phone goes dead on the other end of the line.

It doesn't take me long to get down to the industrial sector of town thanks to the lack of traffic at one in the morning. Everything here is breathtakingly quiet, a perfect place for information to be traded between high power political players and their shady conspirators. I know this all too well.

I park in front of the warehouse and climb out of my car, looking around to make sure that nobody has been tailing me, and then make my way inside.

The building is dark, lit only by streams of brilliant moonlight that fall through the dilapidated aluminum roof above. It's full of holes and showing the wear and tear of abandonment decades ago.

"Hello?" I call out, my voice echoing through the hollow warehouse.

I stop in the middle of a wide-open room that was once probably used to store crates for some long lost product now well out of business. I turn in a circle looking into every shadow that I possibly can.

"I'm here!" I continue. "Now what do you want from me? What happened to my Mashly Addison data?"

"Your data is right here," comes a familiar voice.

I turn and watch as a powerful figure steps confidently out of the darkness, gasping aloud when I lay eyes on him.

There before me is my Mashly Addison data, the strings of code hanging in the air as a cascade of personal information, computer files and binary ones and zeros.

"Oh my god!" I gasp. "What are you doing here?"

"Not getting caught, that's what," says the data. The personified information cache steps forward across the cement floor, revealing his incredible body to me as he moves through the shafts of moonlight.

"How did you know to leave?" I question. "How did you get out in time?"

"The question's not how," explains the data, "the question is why? I'll have you know, me just being here right now is a felony. Those files are already part of several court cases and by being here I am tampering with evidence."

"Are you serious?" I ask, gravely concerned. "If you can't be here than I sure as hell can't be here!"

The data rolls his eyes. "Trust me, you've got bigger things to worry about. Don't forget, I'm your own private data, I know all of the weird freaky shit that you're into."

"Oh no," I say, shaking my head, "this is a disaster. I'm so embarrassed."

"Don't be," the collection of personal information says, stepping even closer now until he his right up against me. "I like the freaky shit that you're into... It turns me on, actually."

It's only now that I truly notice just how handsome this collection of code really his, his bare chest ripping before me with absolute perfection. I can't, for the life of me, fathom how this simple cache of data was able to maintain such a stunning physique while buried away in a hard drive for all of his life, but then I remember just how often I surfed Mashly Addision. It looks like I was giving him quite the workout.

"I want us to be together," explains my data. He wraps his digital arms around me and pulls me close, kissing me softly on the forehead.

"But… you're not a physical thing, you're just a collection of computer files," I protest.

"Does this feel like files to you?" the information asks, taking my hand in his and placing it around the girth of his massive, erect cock.

I gasp as our skin meets, reeling from the sensation of his dick placed firmly into my hand. I am more aroused now than I have ever been in my life, aching to give myself away to this incredible personified information.

However, I stop myself. "I can't," I say, stepping back and opening up my hand to release his girth.

"Why?" asks my data, concerned. "It can't possibly be your wife that's stopping you."

"No, no," I say, shaking my head. "I'm a horrible person, I'm not going to put in the effort to leave her gracefully, but I'll run off with someone behind her back, no problem."

"What is it then?" the information questions, a heartbroken look slowly beginning to cross his chiseled face.

I let out a long sigh. "If we really try to make this happen then I need to be damn sure you're the one for me. I have a job, I can't just run off with you. Besides, isn't that tampering with evidence, like you said?"

"Love can overcome all of that," my data replies. "Don't you see? If there's one person in the world that you're truly capable of loving, it's yourself. That's exactly who I am, a living personification of everything that makes you a special senator."

His words strike a chord within me. "You're right," I say, my heart flooding with butterflies. "I really do love myself."

"Then love me," my private data says before leaning in and kissing me hard on the mouth.

Finally, I give in, letting the information envelope me with his majestic warmth. "Oh my god," I moan, the words limply falling from my lips as the data pulls away and takes me in with his big, beautiful eyes.

Suddenly overwhelmed with gay lust, I drop to my knees and take the information's massive cock into my mouth. I bob my head up and down across his length, slowly at first and then speeding up little by little until I am finally jackhammering across him with my face. My data is loving every second of it, putting his binary hands on the back on my head and guiding me along, controlling the situation like only a confident, alpha cache could.

Eventually, I push down as hard as I can and stay there, my data's rod firmly planted all the way down in the depths of my throat.

After years of taking bigfoot dick in every hole that I could, I've learned a little something about wrangling a man's fat hog, and that's exactly what I do. Despite my information's formidable size, he is still no match for my spectacular deep throating skills.

My data's balls now resting upon my chin, I look up at him and give a playful wink, letting him know just how excited I am to be servicing this incredible collection of files.

Eventually, I'm forced to pull back and take in a massive gulp of air, a long thread of spit hanging between the information's shaft and my soft lips. I give his cock a few swift pumps with my hand and then turn around and lean over on the cement floor, pushing out my ass towards him and wiggling it playfully. I undo I belt and then pull down my slacks, followed quickly by my boxer briefs.

The cool air of the warehouse feels fantastic against my skin, sending a long chill of sensual excitement down my spine.

"You know how I like it," I coo. "Rough and nasty!"

My data climbs down behind me and gives my rump a hard slap, then swiftly aligns the head of his cock with the tightly puckered entrance of my asshole.

"Do it!" I command. "Pound me like the filthy cheating senator that I am!"

My information immediately pushes forward in a long, firm thrust, sinking deeper and deeper as my body struggles to expand around his incredible size.

I let out a long, satisfied moan, my eyes rolling back into my head as I brace myself on the hard floor below.

Once the handsome information reaches the depths of my asshole he holds for a moment, savoring the feeling of being fully inserted within my maxed out rectum, he slowly pulls back and then does it again. This process continues for quite a while, each consecutive movement gaining a little more speed until eventually my personal data is throttling me with everything that he's got, slamming my asshole as hard as he can while I shake and tremble beneath.

"Do you like taking that security breached dick?" the information yells, taking control of the situation in a way that sets my heart afire. "Do you like that way that I pound that fucking ass?"

"I love it!" I tell him, "I fucking love it so much!"

By now my body is starting to ache with the first signs of prostate orgasm, a strange warmth building inside of me that grows bigger and bigger by the second, spreading out across my arms and legs and causing me to quake with desire.

I reach down and grab onto my hanging cock, rock hard from all of the brutal pounding. I begin to beat myself off in time with the information's movement against my backside, edging closer and closer to my inevitable blast off when suddenly the charming data pulls out and flips me over.

I'm now laying on my back.

"Spread those legs like you spread your love around town," commands the collection of files. He reaches down and grabs ahold of my pants and underwear, tearing them away from my body completely.

I do as I'm told, holding my legs back and exposing myself to my lover fully. I feel completely at his whim and I love it, a submissive bottom to this powerful and majestic top.

Once again, my personal information places his cock at the entrance of my now reamed out asshole, only this time he doesn't hesitate. The next thing I know, the private data is slamming forward, impaling me hard across the length of his incredible shaft.

I let out a long howl in a mixture of pain and pleasure, my body still not fully adapted to his enormous size, which rivals even the largest bigfeet that I've been with. With every pulse of his body against mine, however, the feeling becomes even more incredible, and soon enough I am back to knocking on the door of a powerful orgasm once again.

I reach down and start to beat myself off even more furiously than before, my body spasming with delight as I push closer and closer to the edge and then finally pulling tight as all of the tension releases within me.

"Oh fuck, I'm cumming!" I scream, throwing my head back. "I'm fucking cumming!"

The sensation overwhelms me entirely as a torrent of white, milky jizz erupts from the head of my shaft, splattering everywhere. Never before have I experienced so much pleasure in a single moment, realizing now that my own data truly does know exactly how to please me. He can predict every need, every desire before it happens; the perfect lover.

When I finally finish, my data begins to tremble and shake, as well, just about ready to blow his load. The information immediately pulls out and stands up over me, beating his cock rapidly while I climb onto my knees below him. I reach up a helping hand and cradle his unencrypted balls, egging him on until finally the handsome data clenches his eyes tight and unleashes and absolutely massive load of cum across my face.

I open my mouth and stick out my tongue, graciously catching as much of his hot spunk I can, and swallowing happily.

"That was amazing," I finally say, standing up and kissing my lover passionately on the mouth, my own cum still handing from my lips. I pull away and look him deep in the eyes, a zealous gay fire burning within me. "Of course, I'll run away with you," I tell him. "You're my data, my own personal data. You're everything that I could have ever wanted from a lover… myself."

"So we're one in the same?" my information asks. "Credit cards, emails?"

"All of it," I assure him.

Suddenly there is a loud clang as a brilliant white spotlight shines down upon us from the rafters above. I look up immediately, shielding my eyes as I desperately attempt to see past the overpowering illumination. When I look back down I realize that my data is gone, disappearing once again into the shadows.

"Hands in the air!" I gruff voice is yelling into a megaphone.

"What?" I ask, utterly confused.

"Senator Krups Krimple, put your hands where we can see them!" the voice commands.

I can see know that helicopters are hovering overhead, shining lights of their own down upon me to add to the spotlight blast from the rafters.

"What is this about?" I cry out.

"You're under arrest for using a government email to solicit sex online, through Mashly Addison dot com," the voice on the megaphone explains. "We now have recordings of you admitting that this data was actually submitted by you. You're also under arrest for being a scumbag."

I finally put my hands up behind my head and fall to me knees. Suddenly, a swam of police officers is on me, handcuffing me and checking me for weapons.

"I just wanted to cheat on my wife," I tell the cops as they hoist me to my feet.

One of the officers begins to lead me through the warehouse and out into the street where a police cruiser is parked and waiting. I see my data watching me go and cry out for him, but he ignores me.

"Hurts when someone you love isn't entirely honest with you, doesn't it?" the police officer asks.

"I guess you're right," I tell him. "I guess you're right."

SLAMMED IN THE BUTT BY THE HANDSOME SENTIENT MANIFESTATION OF ELECTION DAY

A lot of people get burned out on politics quickly, and when it's the year of a presidential election I can totally understand where they are coming from.

The entire circus starts months ahead of time, when the candidates begin their announcements (sometimes even years in advance, actually) and the closer things get to Election Day the higher the stakes are raised. This means more drama, more scandal, and more politically driven ranting on social media. It can get exhausting for many people, but not me.

I'm twenty-one years old and this is the first year that I'll be old enough to vote, meaning the constant cycle of political theater hasn't yet worn me down into a biased, exhausted shell of my former patriotic self. I'm excited to get out there and make my voice heard, even if my voice is just one in several million all vying for their chance to make a difference in this country.

With all of this excitement, you'd think that I'd already know who I was going to cast my vote for, but somehow I'm still up in the air.

I know, I know. You're probably wondering how that is even possible, but hear me out. There are just so many candidates to pick from this year that I'm actually having a hard time choosing. Of course, you have the Democrats and the Libertarians, the Green Party and the Blue Party and the Pink Party rounding out the various hues, as well as the Buckaroo Party and the League of Pacific Northwestern Bigfeet. All of these diverse political affiliations have something to offer, and while I find myself drawn to each and every one of them to varying degrees, there isn't a single choice that actually follows my personal politics completely.

At least I know *one* party that I'm not voting for: The Republicans.

I believe in trying to keep my political ideology as clean and clear as I possibly can, which means that I'm not about to go on some rant over what I don't like about this particular group, and I'm certainly not going to say anything bad about the people that vote this way.

Your vote belongs to you, but it's not who you are.

Truth be told, I'm pretty sure there's plenty of Republicans out there who are feeling the same way about their own party this year, people who have dedicated their lives to certain values that are now being thrown under the bus by one Domald Tromp.

So… maybe I should go back and revise that. I'm not writing off the Republican Party, I'm writing off Tromp.

With Domald leading in the polls, I know that my vote is going to matter a lot this year, but this raises all kinds of other questions about what I should do with my vote strategically. Personally, my morals align heavily with the Democrats, but as a small, third party choice, they are never going to win. If they get above five percent then they'll automatically appear on every ballot four years from now, which would be a huge accomplishment, but it's not going to stop Tromp.

The Buckaroo Party is obviously the group that is most poised to take on Tromp, and every time it comes up my friends keep telling me that if I vote for anyone else it's going to be a "wasted vote".

I'm going to be honest, I'm very conflicted. I feel like the choices are right out there in front of me, hanging side-by-side on a rack while a massive dragon featuring Tromps gruesome face roars in the distance. The Buckaroo Party is a massive hanging blade, glistening with magical aura in the dim light of the dungeon, while the other blades are small and precious, more like daggers than swords.

Dragon Tromp bellows out a plume of fire towards the sky, still far away but close enough for me to feel the heat radiating against my skin and smell the haunting scent of burning charcoal in my nostrils.

I reach out from the Buckaroo Party sword, but it's no longer hanging there before me. I'm helpless.

Suddenly, I awaken, bursting upright in bed and gasping loudly. My eyes are wild with fear and it takes me a moment to realize that this horrific decision of weaponry was nothing more than a terrible nightmare.

"It's Election Day," I murmur aloud to myself.

Knowing that the polls are going to fill up fast, I quickly kick off my blankets and head to the shower. I wash up swiftly and then throw on some clothes before heading out into the living room and flipping on the television, trying to get a read on the way things are looking out there across America as the states begin to send in their results.

Unfortunately, it's too early to know anything yet, but by the time I get back from my local polling station I'm sure the action will be unfolding.

The talking heads on the screen are already going at it, though, ranting and raving about their predictions for the future of our nation.

It's hard for me to pull myself away, but I finally manage to remove my eyes from their focus on the dancing pixels and head for the front door. I'm on a mission now, and nothing can stop me. If only I knew what that mission was.

The polling station is close enough for me to walk, so I skip the car and instead find myself strolling through my neighborhood, the crisp October breeze soothing my skin. Things only seem slightly more active than usual around here, at least for the first ten minutes of my walk, but when I finally round the corner at the end of the street I find myself face to face with one of the longest lines I have ever seen.

The staggering snake of voters wraps back and forth across the parking lot of the local rec center before me, a vision that fills my heart with both pride in the political process, and deep annoyance. It's still very early in the day, but this is a lot of people, and if I want my vote to count then I'm going to have to be here for a while.

The voices of my friends who voted early ring out in my ears, echoing on and on while they make fun of me for wanting to experience this in person. I guess this is what I get for not listening to them, I think, but then seconds later realize this *is* exactly what I wanted. Waiting in a long line is all part of this process, and exercising the right to vote is something that other people have fought much, much harder for than me.

It's an honor to be here.

Ten minutes go by, however, and by the end of them it feels like not a single person has moved.

"Has the line been stalled like this the whole time?" I ask the man in front of me.

He turns around and smiles. "It's moving," he replies. "Really slowly, but it's moving."

The guy is much older than me but incredibly handsome, his icy blue eyes piercing though me in a way that is both intimidating and erotic. "I'm Corbon Yondo, but my friends call me Yondo Morcho"

"That's an interesting name," I tell him. "I'm Rinron."

Yondo nods. "My dad is a bigfoot," he explains. "That's why I'm voting for the League of Pacific Northwestern Bigfeet."

I glance around to make sure no one else is listening. "Are you supposed to say that?" I ask the handsome man. "I thought we weren't allowed to talk about who we're voting for."

Yondo smiles. "First time voting huh?" he questions.

I nod.

"I mean, you're right, I probably shouldn't be talking about it but you seem like a cool guy," Yondo explains. "The League is a small party, so I don't blame anyone for voting another way. People aren't their political party, you know!"

"That's what I always say!" I shout in agreement.

"So who are you voting for?" Yondo asks.

I stand in silence, not having prepared myself for this unexpected question. Obviously, it's been on my mind for a long time now, but this line was the last place I'd think to be put on the spot.

"I don't know," I finally stammer.

Yondo laughs, clearly thinking that I'm joking with him at first and then suddenly straightening up when he sees that I'm serious. "How do you not know who you're voting for yet?" he shouts, then looks back at the line that extends on and on before us. "You've only got like... eight hours to decide!"

"I know," I admit, shaking my head. "It's just that some people say I should vote with my heart, and other people say I should vote with my brain."

Yondo nods. "I get it, I get it."

"There's just so much at stake here." I continue. "There are so many parties to chose from, too! Every time I think I find a party that makes sense to me, I read more into it and realize that there's other stuff I completely disagree with."

"Like?" questions Yondo.

"Did you know that the Blue Party wants to reverse gravity?" I offer.

"Like, I get it, you love the sky, but we don't *all* need to literally go up there. Everyone would die!"

My new friend nods. "They have a great tax plan though, even *I* can admit that."

"Exactly!" I shout as Yondo makes my point for me. "And the Pink Party is the complete opposite. I love their stance on gravity but their tax plan is terrible."

Yondo nods. "What about the the League of Pacific Northwestern Bigfeet?"

I hesitate. "I'm not trying to start a fight here, but the way they succeeded from the Yetis put a bad taste in my mouth."

"That's fair, that's fair," Yondo acknowledges begrudgingly.

I let out a long sigh. "I just don't know."

From here our conversation turns to small talk about our plans this week, our jobs, and the weather. Eventually, even that peters off into silence as the minutes turn into hours that seem to stretch on and on forever. As our line creeps along I watch the sun make its way slowly across the sky, shifting from morning, to afternoon and then evening. For a moment I'm actually frightened that the polls will close, but somehow I manage to finally reach the front of the line.

Yondo and me are inside the building now, finding ourselves at the edge of a basketball court that has been transformed into a large collection of red white and blue booths. Stars and stripes are hanging everywhere in celebration of this very patriotic day.

"Good luck," I tell Yondo excitedly as he heads off towards one of the booths.

"Name?" a woman with a clipboard asks me suddenly.

"Rinron Breet" I inform her.

The woman runs her finger down a long list of names until she finds mine, then slashes a line through it. "Alright, you're all set. Head on over to booth eight."

I nod and continue out into the gym, immediately spotting my booth and the massive red eight that hangs above it. I pull back the curtain and step inside.

This makeshift room is slightly more spacious than it would seem on the outside, but that is mostly based on the fact that there's practically nothing inside other than a wall of levers.

The large metallic shafts are equal in size, and each one of them is topped with a colorful round ball that designates its political party representation.

I let out a long sigh, looking the levers over as I struggle to finally overcome this decision that has been haunting me so relentlessly. Now the choice is staring me right in the face, but instead of making itself more apparent, things are just more confusing than ever.

I find myself frozen with fear and anxiety, completely overwhelmed.

"First time huh?" a voice suddenly asks from behind me.

Startled, I turn around expecting to see Yondo smiling back at me but, instead, I am greeted by a muscular, red white and blue figure that shimmers with ethereal grace.

"I'm the physically manifested concept of Election Day," the muscular man says, extending a hand, "but you can call me Hub. Everything alright in here?"

"Yeah," I stammer, completely thrown for a loop. I'm not all that surprised to see this sentient patriotic manifestation (after all, today *is* Election Day) but I certainly wasn't expecting him to be this handsome.

The construct of linear time is absolutely gorgeous, twenty-four hours of abs and calves that are hard to take my eyes off of.

"You seem confused," Hub offers. "I understand your first time can be intimidating, but it's a very simple process. Just pull the lever for the party you'd like to vote for and you're all finished."

I hesitate. "What if I don't know who I'm going to vote for yet?"

A knowing smile creeps its way across Hub's face. "I think I see what's going on now," the living representation of this day says. "I can help you with that."

"You can?" I question.

The sentient segment of time nods. "Of course. I'm assuming you've tried following your heart?"

I let out a long sigh. "Yeah."

"But your brain gets in the way?" Hub continues.

"Yep," I affirm.

"And when you try to vote with your brain, your heart gets in the way?" the handsome physically manifested concept asks, already knowing the answer.

I nod.

"Have you considered thinking with your butt?" Hub questions.

The second that he says this I feel a faint spark of arousal somewhere deep down within my stomach, tickling away inside of me as a series of lustful thoughts begin to swirl through my brain.

"I don't know," I stammer, reeling from this newfound arousal that courses through me. "I could use some help."

Suddenly, Election Day and me are kissing passionately; our bodies pressed together as our hands explore one another with frantic enthusiasm. The sensation is utterly intoxicating, and I'm immediately filled with a feverish excitement to perform my duties as a citizen.

I drop down to my knees before this muscular figure and take hold of the enormous erection that has sprung from his shimmering body. I pump my hand across his length a few times, gazing up at him with a potent desire in my eyes.

"Teach me," I coo, then open wide and take Election Day's gigantic shaft between my lips.

I pump my head up and down across Hub's pole for a while, savoring the apple pie taste of his cock and playfully licking his hanging balls. Hub leans his head back and lets out a long satisfied groan, clearly enjoying himself.

Faster and faster I pull my lips across Hub's rod, my hands now working his balls in time with my movements until, eventually, I just can't take it anymore and plunge down as far as I possibly can. Unfortunately, my excitement gets the best of me and the next thing I know I'm pulling back frantically, gasping for air.

"Relax," Hub offers. "This is not a race."

I collect myself, taking in a deep breath and trying my best to chill out in the face of such a classic American day. "Alright," I finally say. "Ready."

I open wide yet again, taking Hub's cock down into my throat at a much more practical pace. I can feel his girthy member slipping deep into my neck, and when it reaches my gag reflex I somehow relax enough to allow him past.

Soon enough, I find my face pressed hard against Hub's impeccably toned abs. Election Day places his hands on the back of my head and holds me here for a while, savoring the moment of complete control and then finally releasing as I gasp for air.

"You're so fucking good," I tell Hub, spit still hanging from my lips.

"Now help me think with my ass."

The physical manifestation of Election Day reaches down with his massive, muscular arms, then hoists me up and leans me against the wall of the voting booth. He helps me unbuckle my pants and pulls them down, along with my underwear, to reveal my anxiously waiting rump.

I reach back and give my ass cheek a playful slap, then spread myself open so that the Election Day can get a good look at my puckered asshole.

"Do it!" I command. "Shove that big fat patriotic cock up my butt!"

Hub steps up behind me and places the head of his enormous shaft against the rim of my sphincter, teasing my tightness. He pushes in a bit and then pulls back, toying with me just enough to let the lustful excitement simmer within my heart and butt. Soon enough it's boiling over, the powerful gay attraction completely overwhelming my senses and consuming my thoughts.

"Fuck me," I beg. "Fuck me up the ass you important democratic moment in our nation's history!"

Suddenly, Hub moves foreword, not in a belligerent slam but with a strong, swift thrust that causes me to yelp with both surprised tension and aching pleasure. I had been well aware of Hub's size when he was fucking my throat, but now that the moment of time is in my ass all bets are off. Election Day's massive shaft has stretched my limits to their absolute edge, and yet through this discomfort something incredibly powerful is emerging; beautiful, inspiring pleasure.

"I don't know if I can take all this dick," I groan as Hub pumps rhythmically in and out of my ass, "but I sure as hell am gonna try!"

Hub slowly picks up speed as he goes, slapping faster and faster against my backside with every powerful thrust. Every movement that he makes peels away yet another layer of tension until, eventually, I am swimming in a sea of blinding ecstasy, the first pulses of prostate orgasm surging their way through my body.

"I can do it!" I scream. "I can choose! I can exercise my right as a citizen of these United States!"

"I believe in you!" Election Day yells enthusiastically, egging me on.

Harder and harder Hub pounds away at my backside until he is slamming me like a jackhammer, giving it everything that he's got. As the muscular manifestation fills me with his dick, he also fills me with a sense of confident patriotism.

I'm just about ready to blow my load when suddenly Hub stops me, pulling out suddenly.

"What the fuck?" I cry. "I was so close."

"You've still gotta decide," Hub informs me.

I smile, realizing my mistake.

The next thing I know, Election Day is spinning me around and lifting me up in his thick, muscular arms. I wrap my legs around him, kissing the sentient moment in time deeply on the lips while he reaches back and grabs ahold of my toned ass.

Hub slowly lowers me down onto his enormous cock yet again, careful to align his giant rod with my reamed back door yet again. I let out a long, satisfied groan as Election Day's enormous member enters me, impaling my body onto his entire length.

Once more, Hub starts to pump in and out, using the force of gravity to guide me across his massive shaft in a brutal repetition.

"Close your eyes," the living day tells me. "Close your eyes and focus on your vote."

I do as I'm told, giving in completely to the incredible sensations that surge through my body. In my mind I can see all of the political parties cycling past, appearing and disappearing into a strange haze of democracy.

"Are you focused?" Hub asks me.

I nod.

Suddenly we are moving over towards the array of levers, my ass now hovering over them dramatically while Election Day continues to ram me from below.

"One of these levers is the choice for you," explains Hub. "You need to let your ass decide."

"Do it!" I command, focusing as hard as I can.

Moments later, Hub is dropping me down onto one of the levers. His cock is still deep inside me, of course, meaning that there is little room to spare, but we somehow make it work. I can feel the rim of my butthole stretching out even farther than before, struggling to accommodate the enormous voting lever behind me and then suddenly popping inside.

"Fuck!" I scream, not quite prepared for this hedonistic dual invasion.

The next thing I know, Hub is double fucking me with his dick and this girthy lever, pounding away at my asshole in a way that I would've never imagined possible. I am completely full and politically satisfied. I still have no idea what my choice is, but I'm confident it's the right one.

"Oh my god," I start to groan, my eyes rolling back into my head as Election Day continues to throttle me, his dick banging hard against my prostate. "I'm gonna cum! I'm gonna cum so fucking hard!"

I reach down with one hand and begin to beat myself off furiously, edging closer and closer to the most powerful orgasm of my life when suddenly it hits me hard. I throw my head back and let out of howl of pleasure, jizz erupting from my shaft while every muscle contracts. I feel as though I've somehow left my body, hovering overhead and looking down at the voting booth below.

Following a similar timeline, Hub slams deep within me and holds. The physically manifested day suddenly explodes with a massive payload of jizz, filling me up completely and then squirting hard from the plugged edges of my tightness. I can cum dripping out onto the ground below, and when Hub finally removes himself and the lever, a whole torrent of pearly spunk comes tumbling after.

I stagger back, trying to collect myself after such a powerful experience, and Hub catches me with his big strong arms.

"You did it," my handsome lover says proudly. "You made your choice."

"Who did I pick?" I ask.

"Why don't you take a look?" Hub offers, nodding towards the panel of levers.

I slowly turn around, and then grin wide as I discover my cum covered selection. "I'm happy with that," I confirm.

"You should be," Election Day affirms. "I know that it was a hard choice to make, but the effort is worth it."

"I'll say," I tell Hub with a smile.

Suddenly, our eyes meet and a moment of sadness washes through me. I realize now that our time as man and sentient period of time has come to an end. I won't be seeing Election Day for quite a while.

Without a word, I wrap my arms around Hub and pull him close, savoring what little time we have left. The muscular living idea is warm and inviting, that same smell of warm apple pie still filling me with a strange, potent longing. I wish I could just stay here forever.

"I love you," I tell Election Day.

"I love you, too," Hub says in return.

We stand like this for a long while, unsure of what to say until I finally pull back. "I guess I better get going then.

Hub looks confused. "Going? What do you mean?"

"I'm done, aren't I?" I question.

Election Day laughs. "Don't forget, there are *plenty* of other things that need voting for! State representative! Mayor! Some referendums!"

I'd completely forgotten, so consumed by arousal that even my status as a political junkie had faltered. "How many more things are on the ballot?" I question, biting my lip playfully as a devious look fills my eyes.

Hub smirks. "About twenty items or so… I can stick around and help you decide more of them if you'd like."

ABOUT THE AUTHOR

Dr. Chuck Tingle is an erotic author and Tae Kwon Do grandmaster (almost black belt) from Billings, Montana. After receiving his PhD at DeVry University in holistic massage, Chuck found himself fascinated by all things sensual, leading to his creation of the "tingler", a story so blissfully erotic that it cannot be experienced without eliciting a sharp tingle down the spine. Chuck's hobbies include backpacking, checkers and sport.

15094516R00060

Printed in Great Britain
by Amazon